Best Things in Life

WALK ON BY

STACEY SOLOMON

Walk on By
ISBN # 978-1-784-303-044
©Copyright Stacey Solomon 2015
Cover Art by Posh Gosh ©Copyright 2014
Interior text design by Claire Siemaszkiewicz
Totally Bound Publishing
Stacey Solomon Management: Total Artist Management

WALK ON BY

Dedication

Zachary and Leighton – The loves of my life. Driving me to succeed in all I do. I love you more than you'll ever know!

Mummy, Daddy, Bubba Solomon – The best parents anyone could wish for guiding me strong and steadily through life! Without you I wouldn't exist! What a terrible thought! Haha.

Jemma and Matthew Solomon – Love u bro and sis always there when I need you and supporting everything I do!

Warren Askew – For being the best manager in the world/ best friend/loser inspiring me and pushing me to be the best that I can be. Always believing in everything that I do! Making it happen no matter what! Nothing is impossible.

Hayley, Harvey, Darcey, Winter and Grayson – I love you all, my extended family.

My Besties (you know who you are)
Love you girls.

Diary

Buskin'

I stood on stage tonight, staring out at the sea of faces, and suddenly it dawned on me that OMG, people were actually listening. They came to see me—me—and it made me think back to the times when I used to busk on the streets, praying that someone would notice me.

Well, tonight they took notice, and it felt so good. I just needed to figure out a way to control this gut-wrenching feeling of fear and anxiety. I was confused—still am—at the conflicting emotions inside me. I've dreamt of stardom since I was little, hoped with all my heart that one day I'd be on stage and everyone would sing my lyrics back to me.

So, anyway, I blinked loads of times while the crowd chanted my name. It felt like every blink lasted a minute or two. I wondered if they thought maybe I'd fallen asleep or was having a seizure. But I didn't care, I needed to zone out, get to that spot (my happy place with my guitar on the station floor) and just sing.

I knew I had to give them what they'd come to hear tonight. Lola. Pretty, sassy, wonderful little Lola. Yep, that's me!

But I do wonder—where is Charlotte? Does she even exist anymore?

My heart hurt from the force of it pounding against my ribcage. My palms excreted more sweat than a comedian in the midst of a high stand-up routine, and my stomach felt like it was literally falling out of my bum!

I closed my eyes and took a deep breath. Instead of the chanting crowd I heard the sound of a train nearing the station. Instead of everyone waiting for a song to come out of my mouth, I pretended they weren't interested—just like

I was invisible when the songs flew out as the commuters walked by.

And, God, it felt like coming home.

1

Oh. My. God!

I have a giant penis in front of me. A. Giant. Penis. In front of me!

I stared at it, wondering what new kind of exciting experience I'd found myself in tonight. Who on earth hosted a party with furniture shaped as body parts? And rude body parts at that! I tried to snap my mouth shut—it had fallen open at my need to giggle—but someone walked past and stuffed a canapé in it.

A tuna canapé. I loved tuna.

I spilled a bit on my clothes so reached for a napkin from the nearest table. After discreetly removing the offending splodge, I glanced around for a bin. There it was—another body part—but this time it was a woman's mouth, all pouty red lips in a selfie smile. *Cute!*

"Wait there a sec," I said to Roo-Roo, my best mate—real name Rupert, like the bear.

He gave me one of his looks—arched eyebrow, big grin—and waved his hand as if wafting away a fly.

"Isn't this a scream?" he, well, screamed.

Yes, it was a bloody scream, something I'd never have thought I'd be a part of in a million years. But as parties were held in places where the walls had seriously big ears, I kept my opinion to myself. If I said one wrong thing, I could find myself in the newspaper come the morning.

"Yeah, it's brilliant," I said, leaving him to stare at the penis-chair in awe while I scooted around a group of chatters to dump the napkin.

The lips of the bin closed around it, and a freakish burp erupted. I jumped and laughed in shock.

I intended to have fun here and it was ages before I had to go home. We'd not long arrived and a crazy night stretched ahead. Someone griped that they wanted to go home and I wondered why they'd want to leave such a madcap bash. Besides, turning up at a party then buggering off after only being there for five minutes wasn't the done thing. It would be a huge snub, and I didn't want to offend anyone.

I went back to stand next to Rupert, feeling lucky I had the chance to make the best of what life had given me. Walk the new path in my sparkly high-heeled shoes and hope I didn't fall over.

I stared at the penis-chair again. I had to admit its curved shape looked comfortable, but to sit on it? Without feeling...odd?

"I bet you love that, don't you?" I said.

Roo-Roo let out a snigger, getting stares from a few people and smiles from others. "Oh, you know how I love a bit of that."

It seemed I'd known Roo-Roo forever. He spent most of his time making celebrities look perfect with his makeup skills. He'd covered spots and blemishes for the best of them, plucked eyebrows—and hairs from moles on chins—so that the public had no idea these icons were actually the same as them underneath the war paint.

Did we all wear a mask? Did anyone else here feel like me? Out of their depth but putting a brave face on it?

Going by the way they were all mingling, dancing and laughing, they were coping just fine.

I flopped onto the chair, hoping to ignore the way-too-phallic design but smacked my cheek against something squishy. Roo-Roo roared, clapping his hands together and rolling his eyes. Turning to see what was so hilarious, I realised how I must look, sitting on a chair of this sort.

Rupert was easily pleased though, bless him.

"Never thought I'd see *that* in my lifetime, sweetcheeks," he said. "Thought you were more of a private girl." He laughed again. "Private. Get it? Penis is a private part?"

I had to laugh. My best friend always knew how to make things better. I was sure he'd sensed when we'd first walked in that I felt like the odd one out, seeing as I was newish to this kind of thing. Yeah, I was relatively new to stardom and still had a lot to learn. I'd daydreamed about being famous, pictured the flashing lights of cameras as I walked the red carpet or smiled for fans as they called my name from the crowd, but I'd never daydreamed about sitting on a huge penis-chair in a room full of people I hardly knew. I'd never imagined it would be seen as absolutely *normal*.

"There's a bum over there, look," Rupert said, pointing across the room.

A sea of famous faces swam in front of me, people I'd watched on TV, and for a second it gave me a shock. I, Charlotte Taylor—or Lola as I was known—was famous too.

Bizarre.

The bum in question was another seat. It was bright pink, of course. Two people were perched on it, drinking champagne and having a good laugh.

Roo-Roo plopped himself onto the head of the penis-chair, his back to me. He loved this kind of party, where he could mingle—and wow, did he mingle. It seemed like he knew everyone, but I'd guessed he would. He'd probably prettied up every face in the room at some time or other. He reminded me of that guy who'd played Christian in *EastEnders*—same kind of looks, same hunky body. The weird thing was, in the months I'd known him, I'd never seen him with a boyfriend. He fancied people all right, told me who he thought was sexy and who wasn't. He just hadn't found the right person.

Like me.

As I sat watching the crowd, sipping my drink, I drifted into a daydream—something I did a lot. While the party continued on around me, I imagined my knight in shining armour walking in, spotting me on this chair—and that wouldn't matter, he wouldn't think it was strange—then coming over and sweeping me into his arms. I could feel my eyes glaze over and I smiled at what I saw in my head.

I'm in my fantasy man's arms, and he carries me outside before lowering me onto a balcony. We're alone and both of us lean forward and rest our arms on the railing whilst staring at the stars. The moon is full – it has to be full because that's romantic – and I get a little thrill when he shifts one hand across the space between us so it touches the side of mine.

"I'm in love with you," he says, voice all gravelly, as though I've stolen his ability to breathe.

With me? He's in love with me?

I could squeal with happiness.

"I knew it as soon as I saw you." He smiles, and the light of the moon brightens one side of his face.

"*Let me rescue you from all this,*" he goes on. "*You're a princess – you don't belong here.*"

I wait for him to say something else.

"*You're so beautiful, Charlotte…*"

I'm just about ready to swoon like a heroine from a regency novel. I'll need to get the smelling salts out in a minute if he isn't careful.

He leans across. Comes so close. Close enough that his breath drifts over my cheek. He smells of toothpaste, and I'm pleased he takes such good care of himself. I hold my breath and wonder if he's going to kiss me. I hope he will – oh, I hope he will.

Anyway, he kisses me, but it's one of those just-about-touch-your-lips kisses, where he has me wanting more. But I hold back. I don't want to come across as a man-eater, do I? And besides, I like men who take charge and do all the running.

He can run to me any day of the week.

"*I want you,*" he says against my mouth.

And oh my God, I'm completely sold.

"*Oh!*" I say, not really knowing what else to do. Plus, I just want to hear his voice, to know what he's going to come out with next.

"*I have a boat on the Thames,*" he says. "*I want to take you there and ravish you.*"

Ravish? *I almost laugh at that, because this is coming from my imagination and even in my head it sounds a bit daft. But if I do it would be rude and spoil the illusion. Instead, I smile and nod, letting him know I'm up for it. What woman wouldn't want to be whisked off to a boat by a man who has Adonis good looks and the makings of a serious charmer?*

He takes my hand and leads me back through the crowded party room. As we breeze past Roo-Roo, he stares at me with his eyes wide, his mouth in an 'O' of shock. He mouths, "Who's that man?" but I don't have a chance to reply. Mr

Perfect guides me towards the door, and within seconds I'm out of there, standing in the foyer.

"Your coat, lovely lady?" he asks.

"I didn't bring one," I manage, my voice coming out as a whispery choke. I lift my hand to my throat, fiddling with my diamond necklace, like so many heroines do. I sigh — Yes! I'm so getting into this! *— and wish he'd kiss me again, right here, right in front of the few people who chat by the stairs.*

"What on earth is wrong *with you, girl?" he says.*

I blinked. That voice didn't sound like my Mr Right.

Roo-Roo's face was inches from mine. He stared at me, a frown firmly planted on his forehead, the creases three rows of wiggly lines.

I jumped, which had me sliding off the seat. I scrabbled to stay on it but I was sliding fast, trying not to laugh my head off. "Oh, bloody hell, Roo-Roo!" I said, coming out of my daydream way too fast for my liking.

I slipped until I landed on the floor beside Rupert and was treated to the sight of a multitude of stiletto sandals and painted toenails.

Lovely.

"Oh, let me help you up," Rupert said, extending his hand. "You look so funny down there. Don't worry about what people might think. You fit *right* in. They'll just think you're as pissed as a fart."

Face flushing, my cheeks getting hotter by the second, I took Roo-Roo's hand. He helped me to my feet, and I glanced around to see who'd noticed my slide of shame.

No one, it seems.

Thank God for that, but, I hadn't finished with my imaginary man yet. He was waiting to take me to his boat. We were meant to be running off to his car — which would be a sporty little number, maybe red, maybe black—then zooming into the night towards the Thames, the lights twinkling on the surface, everything super cool in my world.

"You were staring at nothing," Roo-Roo said. "Really staring, darling."

I smiled to show him I was okay. The last thing I wanted was him flapping in a panic around me. He could get a bit protective and sometimes stifled me, but I loved him all the same.

"I must have been daydreaming," I said. "Silly me!"

And as sad as it was, I wanted to be doing it again. Letting out random, movie-like giggles with Mr Studly as we clambered onto his boat. Me majorly excited because he wanted to 'ravish' my body. Him going all masculine and ripping my clothes off, the buttons of my dress flying, pinging against the walls. Oh, I was in danger of zoning out again.

"Stop it," Roo-Roo said. "You're doing it again. The staring thing." He pursed his lips. "Listen, I don't think you're very well. Pop yourself back down and I'll get you a glass of water."

He swanned off, and I turned back to the offending chair but someone else was already there.

Deborah Cressida, aka Bitcherella. The one woman most people dreaded seeing at every party. And she was at *every* party. Think long, straight black hair— perfect hair. Cat-like eyes.

I smiled at her.

She smiled back.

"Still attending parties with your gay sidekick?" she asked, twirling her champagne glass by the stem. "*Surely* you should have a man of your own by now. You're famous, sweetie, you can have anyone you want."

I didn't quite know what to say in response to that so said nothing for a moment. Speaking out of turn to Deborah would be akin to signing my own death warrant. She had her fingers in a lot of pies, and I didn't need her particular brand of meddling in my life. She could ruin a career as quick as you could blink because she apparently sold celebrity stories to the newspapers.

"Maybe I do have a man of my own," I said.

She widened her eyes. "Oh, *do* you now. Come and tell me all about him." She patted the vulgar chair, her red nails catching the light from the chandeliers.

Roo-Roo came our way with a bottle of Evian in his outstretched hand, saving me from going further into that conversation.

"Here," he said, handing the bottle to me, then giving Bitcherella a glare that said two words. One began with F, the other with O. "Let's go somewhere a bit more appealing, shall we? It smells around here."

He started leading me away, and I caught a glimpse of Deborah as she gaped at him for being so rude. People didn't tend to walk away from her. No, they hung around until she'd finished with them, otherwise she'd pitch a fit and make their lives very uncomfortable. Although I'd been famous for about a year now, I was still learning how to handle people like her.

I turned away and followed Rupert, all the while waiting for the fit to be pitched.

Oddly, she didn't sling a nasty parting shot our way.

On the other side of the room, I stood against the wall with Roo-Roo on my left and another bum on my right. This time it appeared to be an ice cream machine, shiny silver, the bum a sculpted piece of art with a waist and the tops of thighs. Waffle cones were stacked next to it, and the handle was set into the base of the back. It was outrageous but it made me giggle.

I dread to think what will come out of that…

I switched my attention from the bum to Bitcherella. She'd moved away and was chatting up a footballer. Some said she was desperate to become a WAG, and one lady had mentioned that Deborah had tried it on with so many footballers but they'd all slipped out of her desperate clutches.

She rubbed his arm—poor guy looked uncomfortable—then glanced my way. She smiled as if to say, 'This is how you do it. This is how you snare a man.'

I didn't want to snare a man. What I wanted was for a man to snare me.

I wanted my dream lover, but there was no chance of thinking about him now, and if Roo-Roo caught me looking all distracted again, he'd cart me off home.

"I'm just going to take this all in for a second," I told him, trying to put his fears about me to rest. "You know what I'm like. It takes me a while to get used to these parties, although I should be well used to them by now."

"All right, darling," he said, patting my arm. "You do that."

I people-watched, but it wasn't long before the usual happened when I was so far out of my comfort zone. I started thinking about the differences in my life now that I was famous. The feeling I'd had the other night when I'd been on stage summed it all up.

I was no longer people-watching. I stared at nothing. Wondering, wondering, wondering about life.

And most of all, I wondered where Charlotte Taylor was slowly disappearing to—and what I was going to do about it.

I stood outside by the pool. Roo-Roo had respected my need for a bit of alone time—if you could call being with a load of people alone—and was inside chatting up a storm and prancing around in his usual manner. My boy was on form tonight.

I needed to learn to let go, to become a star in all respects. To be Lola, the other side of myself, the side that was showbiz—fun and amazing and happy. The side that I would tuck away again once I got home if I felt like it. There I could be Charlotte, the girl from East London who used to get her sweets from the local corner shop, and fly high on the swings in the park.

Taking a seat in a nearby corner of the garden, I sipped my water and watched what was going on. The pool was undoubtedly heated, what with several people cavorting in it with no clothes on—another shocker I'd quickly come to accept, that some people thought nothing of stripping down to their birthday suits and dive-bombing in.

I smiled. They were so crazy and their laughter and antics were infectious, even if they weren't 'normal' to me. For me, normal was being with my family. Kicking back in the comfort of home, laughing about the stuff we used to do when I was a kid. It didn't seem as though I was an adult already. At times I still felt younger than I was. *Why is that?* Why didn't being an adult come with a manual? And why didn't anyone ever tell you that even though you were grown, you still had the same fears that you had as a kid?

A huge splash sent droplets of water into the air. Some landed on my feet, but I ignored them. I was too busy staring in wonder at who was emerging from beneath the surface. Oh, it was the host's pretty girlfriend, Anjellika—and yes, she spelled her name just like that—a tanned goddess he'd met at a nightclub. She was famous for hanging around with the famous. That was okay, if that was her form of happy.

It took all sorts to make a world, as my dad often said.

The host, Johnny—Johnny Bravo in my head— strutted out from the house in his gleaming white suit to stand beside the pool. He wasn't blond like the cartoon Johnny, but he had the same hairdo, all greasy quiff like he thought he was Elvis or something. He wore aviator sunglasses whatever the weather—and inside too—maybe to stop himself being blinded from the glare of his teeth. He was Tango-tanned, seriously orange, and I often thought of him running round slapping people, turning them orange too, the same as on the TV advert.

I shouldn't have been surprised at his body-part furniture, and I shouldn't have been surprised at the size of his pool and the size of the things in his house. He had what some might call small-person syndrome, and everything around him was massive to compensate. 'Hey, look at my things so you don't see I'm height impaired.' A woman had once implied he wore high block heels, too, but his trouser hems were always long so I could never get a proper look. Now, if I could only see him sitting with one leg crossed over the other, my curiosity would be appeased. It had been rumoured in the tabloids that he had his shoes made especially and thought nothing of paying a thousand or more for a pair.

That would make my dad go into one of his rants. *'Bloody hell, I could get a pair that look exactly the same for twenty quid.'*

I smiled. Johnny started posing, throwing his shoulders back and his chest out. His shirts were open at the top all the time, and curly chest hair spilled out. Many women fancied him, but he wasn't my cup of tea — which hadn't helped when he'd approached me once and had made it clear he'd expected me to go to bed with him.

Much as he was a nice enough man, if a bit too saucy, I didn't want to go anywhere with him.

"Quite the splash, babe," he shouted at Anjellika, getting titters in response from almost everyone in the garden.

I grinned at that, because she was quite a splash, so pretty and graceful.

Johnny's voice seemed to still be reverberating around the garden. He shouted a lot. Never a quiet word from him — unless he was trying to seduce you. And although he was nice, Johnny wasn't a man I wanted as an enemy. He could break my career into tiny pieces if he had a mind to — which was why I'd come to his party in the first place. He got offended easily. I hadn't been able to cry off by telling him I was ill because I'd seen him earlier in the day.

I'd come out of the recording studio, and there he'd been, chest on show, sunglasses hiding his roving eyes. I'd been laughing at something my manager, David, had said, so obviously I wasn't ill, obviously I was bright as a button.

Sometimes fate played a mean hand, but then again, the party was great, so I was glad I'd come.

Anjellika scrambled out of the pool, all arms and long legs, her makeup still perfect. If that had been me, my mascara would be running down my cheeks and I'd maybe have a set of false eyelashes sticking to my chin. Even though she'd scrambled, she'd done it in such a way that she still looked elegant. I needed to learn how to do that too.

Anjellika didn't fling herself at Johnny, probably because he'd joke about her getting his suit wet. She stood next to him with one hip cocked, her whole body on show and I could tell she was enjoying the fact that loads of men were staring at her. Johnny was too.

Would I ever be comfortable doing something like that? I doubted it, but maybe I could daydream about myself in the buff — with my fantasy man.

I'd wait until I got home, though. There was still so much to see and do here tonight.

"The music's starting in a minute, babe," Johnny said loudly then flashed her a massive grin. "So go and get yourself dressed. Wouldn't want The Bombastics forgetting their lines once they cop a load of your tits."

Anjellika sashayed off, several blokes staring at her peachy backside. I had a thought then. Did she have the usual women's insecurities, where she worried about a visible panty line? Did she ever wonder how she'd get away with wearing a low-cut dress and no bra without resorting to that special boob tape? Maybe she had a see-through Wonderbra. Even though she was thin — had to be close to a size zero — did she ever feel fat?

I did. Not to the point that I'd change my eating habits. Oh, I might lose a few pounds here and there for a photo shoot, but I liked my food too much to over-worry.

"Come on then, you lovely lot," Johnny bawled. "Get yourselves in the basement." He jerked a thumb in the direction of the house and treated everyone to another spectacular view of his teeth.

Everyone rose as one. I got up too but waited for the others to go inside before I followed. I'd made the mistake before of running with the herd and had had my bum pinched and my boob squeezed for my trouble. Goodness me, that had been an eye-opening experience!

Inside, there was a bottleneck of people at the doorway that presumably led to the basement. The strains of a guitar being twanged filled the air as well as the raspy *shh* of a snare drum and the tapping of a finger against a mic. The excited hum of chatter gave the impression that I was waiting to see my favourite group with other fans at a rock concert, and I realised people felt this way when coming to see me on stage.

Wow. Surreal much?

It made me want to do what I did best—sing.

"Lola!" Roo-Roo called, waving maniacally from the other side of the foyer, only his head visible over the crowd. "Wait for me!"

Oh, I'd be waiting for him all right. No way did I want to go down those steps without him—I loved having my best friend with me. I waved back then moved to stand near the wall so everyone else could shuffle along without me being in their way. Female laughter wafted past me—as did Deborah and the scent of her perfume. It smelled lovely. She clung to the footballer she'd been chatting to earlier as though her life depended on it. He didn't seem as uncomfortable as he had before, but alcohol had a habit of easing out the kinks. He just had to hope any kinks he had with her later didn't end up as printed text for all the world to see. I really hoped the rumours about her running to the press with tales weren't true and that she could find happiness with a good man.

She disappeared downstairs, seeming contented and relaxed.

Roo-Roo pushed through the throng to come and stand beside me. "Oh, you should have been inside just now, darling," he said, holding one hand up and twirling his wrist, finger pointed to his temple, showing me something crazy had happened. He leaned close. "Deborah has had a little too much to drink and…" He paused—for effect, I knew. "She simulated" —he said it as *symoolated*—"having sex with that willy chair."

"Oh, my God," I said. "She didn't!"

"She jolly well did, dear." Roo-Roo beamed a wide smile, clearly enjoying telling me about it. "She looked positively *filthy*! Like some girl on heat." He shuddered violently. "I wouldn't want to be that footballer tonight. She has nothing but one thing on her mind, that one. Money, honey, not sex." He rolled his eyes and plonked one hand on his hip. "And don't we just *know* what will happen if he goes to *bed* with her?"

"Aww, I hope things work out for her. Everyone deserves happiness."

"Give it a couple of days," Roo-Roo said, "and he'll be wishing he'd never had that last bottle of beer. He's just got to hope his manager doesn't see it as the last straw." He gave me a knowing smile. "Because the whole of London is waiting for Mr Fancy Pants of the Field to mess up again."

Mr Fancy Pants—I liked that name. It suited him. He always wore the best clothes, looked well-groomed *all* the time, and acted like a bit of a Casanova. He was single, had been for ages, so I didn't think it was anyone else's business who he slept with.

The crowd at the door had almost gone. Only one or two people lingered in the foyer, so I followed Rupert down the stairs. The walls either side of the steps were made to look like grey rock, as though we were entering a cave. Spotlights brightened the way, casting thin beams back and forth in a criss-cross effect. It was all a bit unreal.

"Here comes the fun, petal," Roo-Roo said. "Almost down there."

We reached the bottom quickly. I stared around at the basement. Yeah, it was basically a cave, with water dribbling down the walls into a tiny stream that circled the room. The stream was lit from beneath with lights of all colours, and a current carried the water along, creating the illusion of a wavering rainbow.

I wondered if I'd get my ultimate pot of gold at the end of my rainbow. My dream fella, standing there with his muscled arms, waiting for me to run into them where I'd feel safe and loved and...*oh, don't go there. Do not start with the daydreams.*

I tagged behind Roo-Roo as he elbowed his way through the crowd, which was pretty big. Bodies were packed close together, just like at a concert, and we made it to the front. I loved The Bombastics. They were new and fresh, one of Johnny's friend's creations, plucked from playing in clubs to playing on the big stage. I liked them so much because they were excited and honoured that their dreams had come true.

The music started and I had the familiar feeling I always got—the feeling of being free. The band belted out their current hit, and a cheer went up. A rush of excitement went through me that I was here experiencing such a great atmosphere. People danced — some of them from the pool were still naked — while others swayed or tapped their feet.

Roo-Roo looked across at me and winked, then danced like he always did, exuberantly and with a lot of arm waving. I laughed, joining in, embracing everything put in front of me as though it was nothing. Dad had always said life was for living, to get out there and enjoy it while you could, so I was determined to give it a good go. I let my muscles relax, danced like there was no tomorrow and, wow, I was so happy.

3

I was struck by indecision. Did I run off home and pretend I wasn't seeing what I was seeing, or did I stay and pretend I knew *all* about it—that I dug the scene but chose not to indulge?

I was standing in a bathroom just off the basement cave. It was much like a public loo, only cleaner, posh, and with a row of toilets in cubicles opposite me. Adjacent to them, to my right, were sinks set in mega expensive, gold-threaded white marble, the taps—you guessed it—gold body parts.

Somehow, I didn't much fancy washing my hands with water that jetted out of man-bits.

Three skinny models stood in front of the sink unit. One blonde, two dark-haired. The blonde was bent over the marble top surrounding the sinks, the ends of her long hair puddling on the counter. Her skin-tight, black sequinned dress emphasised her lack of weight. Roo-Roo would have said she needed a bit of meat on her bones.

The other two watched her, clearly waiting their turn. Their dresses were similar, except one was red, the other royal blue. Very pretty and they suited the women. Maybe they'd been given them from a new line of clothing they'd modelled—lucky ducks! Whoever had designed them mustn't have thought covering nipples was an option, though. The front sections, although still coloured, were transparent, leaving nothing to the imagination. *Oh la la!*

A loud sniff, then Blondie stood upright. She turned to stare at me, smiled and beckoned me over with a hand that held a wide, stubby straw.

Did she nick that from the burger bar?

"No thanks," I said, plastering a big grin on my face then making my way, on legs shaking like jelly, to one of the toilets. I wasn't about to judge. What they put in their bodies was their business. "But you have a good time there…"

Once I'd locked myself in the stall, I hung my little black bag from a hook on the door. I took a minute to get my breathing back to normal. It had quickened and my heart had gone all daft on me, throwing out crazy, throbbing beats. I sat on the closed toilet lid, hoping the other two models would sniff quickly then get out so I could use the loo. I didn't want to have to face them once I'd finished my business. Didn't want the pressure of being coaxed into doing what they were doing.

"Hurry up," one said. "I want mine."

She sounded on edge, as though it had been ages since she'd had a hit. I recognised the signs of people on drugs pretty well now, having seen so many who were into that stuff. It was a sad state of affairs, and bloody hell, I wanted nothing to do with it.

"Shut up and wait your turn," said another.

"I'll do it when I'm good and ready."

She was obviously *really* ready. A humungous, loud sniff echoed around the bathroom. I cringed, wishing I hadn't come in.

"You know," the first one said, "if you take too much of that, your dress size is going to go into the minus."

I could agree with that. Already they wore zeroes, that much was obvious. I'd seen those three around a lot before at parties, always together. Someone, somewhere along the way had told them to aim for their current body size.

That someone was totally wrong.

While another hefty intake of air ricocheted off the black tiled walls, I sat and thought about the amount of food they must waste. At a dinner once, I'd seen them wolfing down massive meals then, straight after, scarpering to the ladies' room. I secretly called them The Snorters—that's what they did in the toilets, so Roo-Roo had been told.

I'd asked him once whether he gossiped about me to people, and he'd looked at me, horrified that I'd suggested such a thing. But I'd only known him a couple of weeks at the time and hadn't been sure who to trust back then. Now, because nothing I'd ever told him so far had made it to the rumour mill, I thought I could tell him anything.

While I waited, I remembered how we'd become such good friends. He'd done my makeup for a chat show I was appearing on and we'd hit it off right away. Afterwards, he'd been in the green room and, when I'd walked in shaking from head to toe, he'd been the only one to come up to me and ask if I was okay. That had led to us having coffee together, then to meeting up for lunch the next day, then a movie night at my house the following week. The rest, you could say, was history.

Thinking of him made me realise I needed to get out of the bathroom. Now. He'd be worrying over how long I'd been in here—especially if he'd seen The Snorters come in before I had.

My other close friend, Indecision, perched on my shoulder and I wished my sister, Jenna, was perched there instead. She'd know exactly what to say, tell me exactly what to do. She was a glass-half-full kind of person and always told it like it was. No beating around the bush, she just came out with things and her advice was usually spot on.

What would she say to me now? Think. Think!

"Get up, go out there, wash your hands, and pretend you didn't hear them if they speak to you, then make yourself scarce." That's what she'd advise.

Go on, you can do it…

I took another deep breath then stood, still bursting for the loo because I hadn't got around to that yet. I collected my bag and hung it over my shoulder. Then I opened the door and peeked out before leaving the stall. The Snorters were on their second line, so while they were busy I washed my hands—in case they thought I *had* done my business—then held them under the obscene drying machine. The pink thing, shaped like a gigantic boob, blasted out an excessively violent burst of hot air from the nipple. It hit me in the eyes full force, and I let out a strangled, "Argh!" while staggering and slipping around the bathroom, blinking in an attempt to see straight. I blundered into something soft yet hard, blinked again then, once my vision finally cleared, realised I'd knocked into one of The Snorters.

She stood there with her hands on her non-existent hips, giving me what I assumed was the evil eye.

"Oh, God, I'm *so* sorry," I said, tears streaming down my face. I swiped them away with the back of my hand. I was surprised I'd been able to speak—the air had also dried my mouth out and my tongue felt as though I'd walked through a cloud of deodorant.

"I didn't mean to do that. You know, knock into you. It was that thing's fault. As you probably saw, the air smacked me in the face when it came out of the nipple and I couldn't see and I had to get away from it and I…" I shut my mouth.

They stared at me, faces full of thunder — if thunder could look like anything — then burst out laughing. Talk about giving off confusing signals. And why were they laughing now when before they'd seemed just about ready to start a slanging match? Had my hair-do gone all messy or something? I didn't think I'd said anything funny. Mortified at my faux pas, I made a move to leave, but the blonde grabbed my wrist.

"Come on, have some of this," Blondie said, tipping her head to one side, indicating a line of what I assumed was coke. "It'll make you feel better. You're way too anxious."

"No, really, I'd rather not."

"Okay, so you don't want any speed, fine, but fucking hell, you're hilarious," Blondie said. "When that air came out your…your…" She slapped a bony hand onto the marble then doubled over, chortling.

I had the alarming thought that she might snap in half, bless her.

Still, I could see the funny side of what had happened so I giggled with her, relieved she wasn't going to push me on the drugs issue.

"Listen," she said, her voice going up an octave as she tried to get herself under control, "have you ever thought about modelling?" She pointed at my body.

Self-conscious alert!

I glanced down at my size ten self, feeling overweight next to them and, under such intense scrutiny, I wished the floor tiles would slide apart and reveal a set of stairs that I could escape down.

"You ought to think about doing a bit of runway work," the black-haired one said, sizing me up and circling her finger and thumb around my wrist. "Yes, you just about pass the chunky test."

Chunky test?

To prevent myself from asking her to elaborate, I had a good nose at her. She had a severe-cut bob, her fringe — halfway up her forehead — as straight as a ruler edge. Her eyebrows were the shape of arrow heads, their centres pointing to her hairline.

"Oh, I couldn't do that," I said, knowing that if I did I'd maybe fall arse over tit the moment I started walking down the runway. I wasn't made for strutting my stuff like they were.

And why would they think I could do that when a bit of hot air had the ability to take away my motor skills? They channelled air at you on those kinds of jobs to create the illusion the wind was blowing, didn't they? Going by the size of those fans, I'd be lifted off my feet and thrown back the way I'd come.

"Yeah, you could do that," Arrow Eyebrows said. "I know who your manager is. I'm going to talk to him about it. Great exposure, great for your career. Just think of how you'd feel in a fabulous dress and high heels, gliding down the runway."

That was something I most definitely *didn't* want to think about, how I'd feel on the runway. I giggled as a response. They smiled widely at me, probably thinking that was my way of saying yes. They seemed like they were struggling not to laugh again.

"Oh, I'm so pleased you're up for it." Arrow Eyebrows engulfed me in a hug.

She let me go and smiled to herself. I wondered if maybe one day we could be friends. I didn't have many these days, and being able to chat to a female about girly things would be so nice.

"Well," I said brightly, "that's really lovely of you to have such confidence in me. And yes, speak to my manager, if you want." I made a mental note to warn him they'd be in contact and to let him know I most definitely did *not* want that particular job. I could only hope he agreed with me, that it wasn't something I *should* involve myself with. But, as he only wanted what was best for me, if he thought it was a good idea I participate, I'd consider it.

"Oh, goody!" Blondie said, jumping up and down on the spot. "Right, girls, one more hit then it's time to party!"

I smiled again then left them to it, rushing out of the bathroom. After finding Roo-Roo in the middle of the crowd, bouncing around in a demented fashion, I told him I was going home. Tiredness had come over me suddenly.

"So soon, petal?" he shouted into my ear.

"I'm tired," I said, offering an apologetic smile that he might not be able to see in the semi-darkness. The lights had been turned down while I'd been acting a complete idiot in the bathroom.

"Let me make sure you get into a taxi," he said, grabbing my hand and leading me towards the stairs.

In the foyer, he studied my face. "Uh, darling?"

"Yes?" I anxiously fiddled with my bag strap.

"You have an eyelash attached to your earlobe. It doesn't look quite right there. Belongs on your eye, yes?"

I *knew* something like that had happened. And The Snorters hadn't told me. So were they laughing at me again now? At me thinking I had a chance as a runway model? And to think I'd thought we could be friends.

I left Johnny Bravo's party with a heavy heart.

Diary

I Am Confusion Dot Com

Just because money has come into my life, it doesn't mean I'm going to change. But I'm determined to enjoy my new life and whatever it brings.

Earlier, I was sitting in a posh restaurant with more pieces of cutlery beside my plate than those in the kitchen drawer, and it got me thinking about the past and how different it was compared to now. Has having the mass amounts of cutlery and minuscule meals restaurants serve made me any happier? Things are easier, I know that much. I worry less about money and can afford to eat more if I want to. But is that happiness?

Happiness is family. Happiness is me sharing a bed with Jenna, top to tail, and her shoving her feet in my face while she fidgets in her sleep. Happiness is Dad saying he can find a better bargain at the corner shop we used when I was a kid—no need to spend that much, he used to say, when you can get it for a few quid less.

I often think about that little stumpy man, Abdul, the owner. He's always happy. Always smiling and has a good word for everyone who goes there.

He's not rich but he's happy.

I feel so strange! What is wrong with me lately? Why am I thinking about my old corner shop and my sister's cheesy feet? Maybe I just need a little break. Some rest. A holiday. Some time alone so I can think of nothing—nothing at all.

That's it! I'm ringing David and letting him know I'll take him up on his suggestion that I have a break. It's been a long year so far.

Where shall I go?

America? The Big Apple?

Yeah. NYC—bagels, Broadway and blissful emptiness, here I come!

Happy Rocks!

So I can't go to The Big Apple until after the modelling job, which isn't for a while. David thinks it will be good for me to be seen.

I'd say ☹ but will turn that frown around and stay positive. ☺

So I'll be seeing the lovely snorters again soon. Maybe even sharing the runway with them. And most definitely attending the after-party.

I wish my suitcase was overloaded with Charlotte clothes and I was preparing to fly off to NYCeeeeeee, but that's not going to happen yet, so I need to pull up my big girl pants and get on with it.

I'm off to a music award ceremony tonight—I'm up for best newcomer YAY! ☺ There is such an amazing amount of talent in the category, but David said I have a good chance of winning, and I'm just so chuffed to have been nominated anyway. I'm also gonna be singing my latest single. Although it's nerve-wracking before I open my mouth, once I do, everything's all right in my world.

I have a lot to be thankful for and will enjoy everything that comes my way. I must be more like Jenna, who, for the most part, thinks everything has a silver lining.

Talking of Jenna, she rang me this morning to tell me about a woman she's been looking after. The old woman died. Gutted for Jens. She was there to hold her hand, though, when she passed over because there was no one else.

How sad is that? Can't imagine not having even one family member by my bed when my time comes. Okaaaaay, nuf of the sad stuff!

So she didn't feel like a massive pile of poo poo pi doop, I said we'd get together soon and have a good laugh. She cheered up at that, which made me happy too.

Happy rocks!

My dress was the kind I'd only ever dreamt of wearing when I used to think about being famous. There were times I'd browse catalogues or stare through shop windows, imagining myself as the model or mannequin, looking glorious in the frothy creations for sale.

Frothy wasn't exactly in fashion at the moment, though, it was more the sleek sheath dresses that clung to the body and showed off every flaw.

Roo-Roo assured me I didn't have a muffin top, yet I could see it. But I had my hold-it-all-in knickers, and the shop assistant had assured me that they'd *'hide all your extra layers and make you look and feel a million dollars.'*

I stared at the knickers, which I'd laid out on my bed beside the black strapless, backless dress.

Strapless. Backless.

It would mean either wearing a special bra or using The Boob Tape instead.

The Boob Tape option was the winner. My breasts, when I wasn't wearing a bra, were quite big, so they had a tendency to need the extra help of being held in place, so not wearing a bra or tape wasn't an option.

The super knickers were a shade of beige, presumably meant to match my skin tone. Thank goodness my dress didn't have slits up the sides, back or front. *That would be a bit of a disaster, wouldn't it?* Knickers on show for all the music world to see. Nice.

Now, how am I meant to get them on? They looked as though they'd fit a ten year old. I knew they were elasticated but…

Well, I'd soon find out.

I held them up. Turned them this way and that while I convinced myself I'd get the buggers on without much trouble. And get them on I would, considering what they promised to achieve. When I got up on stage – in front of the cameras that would beam my image onto TVs up and down the UK – I couldn't stand to have the muffin issue to contend with as well as my nerves.

If only people knew what Lola really felt like inside…

Scrap that, it was probably best they didn't. Their illusions would be shattered, because, like I'd done in the past, I'd put my idols on a super-high pedestal and wouldn't have been able to bear it if they'd fallen off.

I thought about my acceptance speech and decided not to try battling with the pull-me-in knickers yet. I had a little time to read through the speech one last time to make sure I hadn't forgotten anything – or anyone. I tossed my pants back on the bed then went to my bedside table where the sheet of paper with all my thanks on it, sat waiting.

I picked it up, my eyes misting as I read what I'd written earlier.

God, I was glad I hadn't had my makeup done yet. Roo-Roo would have had a fit if he'd made me look pretty and I'd ruined all his hard work.

In the bathroom, I washed my face with cold water. I stared in the mirror above the sink and saw exactly what I didn't want to see – blotchy skin, red-rimmed eyes and a scarlet-tipped nose. There was nothing for it but to stop this silly nonsense and tuck my emotions away. No room for sentiment before a makeup sesh.

I went back to the bed and the knickers. I couldn't put it off any longer. What if I couldn't get them on and I needed to find something else that would do the same job? If I couldn't do that, I'd need to phone around and get a new dress, one that wasn't so tight.

I checked the label — these pants were so small, I was doubting my body's ability to squeeze into them — and realised that I'd bought the wrong size. Cursing to myself, and knowing I had to at least give it a go, I sat on the bed and began pulling them up my legs. It was going well until they reached my knees and I stood up. They gripped my legs together and weren't going to be letting go any time soon. I rolled the waist and belly part into a sausage shape so I could get better leverage as I tugged some more. They shifted a little higher and, pleased with myself, I congratulated my efforts with a smile of triumph. This was going to be easy.

I tugged them again. It took a good two or three minutes of me huffing and puffing and getting hot-faced and sweaty, but I managed to draw them up a couple of inches higher. This time they got stuck mid-thigh. I relaxed my fingers, flexing them as they'd started cramping. Maybe the material needed to stretch a tad after every attempt. I tried to prise my legs apart to do just that, but they wouldn't budge, not even an inch. They were stuck fast together. The waistband, which I named Hotdog Harry, dug into my skin.

Someone rang the doorbell.

"Oh, hell!"

What was I supposed to do now? It was clear that I didn't have time to pull them all the way up so I had a go at taking them off. They wouldn't move.

"Hang on," I called cheerily, hoping that whoever was at the door would hear me.

They knocked again.

"Oooh, bloody hell!"

I put on my dressing gown then hopped to my bedroom door, conscious that my upper half seemed to have a mind of its own and kept leaning forward. I righted myself, not fancying lurching over. Out on the landing, I bounced a metre or so to the top of the stairs then stopped.

How was I going to do this? Hop down or slide down?

This time, the person rang the doorbell – repetitively.

"Hang on!"

I'd have bent my knees if I could, but that feat was impossible. So I took hold of the banister rail while I let my feet slide along the landing until I was sitting, legs straight out in front of me. Swinging my legs around so they pointed down the stairs, I stared at the carpet and braced myself.

This was going to sting – but it might even be fun.

With one almighty push on the top step, I launched myself downwards. My bum bashed each step, giving my spine a good jolt.

"Ow ow ow ow ow."

"What did you say?" someone shouted.

A man. It was a man!

Was he peering through my letterbox? I squinted to see better, my view of the front door jarring with every bump. I was sure I could see a pair of eyes through the slot. Oh, God, what if it was the press?

"Won't be a second!" I replied, voice juddering, bum burning.

"What the hell are you *doing*? Re-enacting your childhood or what, babe?"

I thought I knew the voice but it was muffled so I couldn't be certain, but I thought it was…

No.

No, no, no.

Johnny Frigging Bravo?

I hit the last step with a particularly hateful thump then smacked onto the hardwood floor. My spine couldn't take any more and neither could my pride. Embarrassment paid an unwelcome visit to my cheeks, and they roared as hotly as my backside, which I was sure must be minus a layer of skin.

No need to exfoliate in the shower later, then.

"Open the door so I can see your… If you're all right," Johnny said.

Like I was going to do that! I had no knickers on – not counting the squash-me-to-death knickers – and I was so glad I'd put my dressing gown on because if Mr Bravo had got an eyeful of me without it, I didn't think I'd ever have lived it down. And I didn't think he'd stop at just looking either. His roving eye was famous – or eyes, the pair of them were naughty – and if I'd thought he'd come on to me before, I had a feeling this time he'd double his efforts. Triple them.

"I'm fine, thank you," I said, seeing him still peering through the letterbox. I guessed he was raising his eyebrows, because his eyes went a different shape.

"You don't look fine. Well, that's a lie, you always look fine, but you know what I mean."

"What are you here for?" I asked, keeping one hand on my robe belt and resting my other arm across my boobs. I was anxious for him to go away so I could sort myself out. "Was it for anything special?"

"I can give you special," he shouted, his eyes narrowing, giving me the idea he was concentrating.

It was then I realised he didn't have his sunglasses on. He must have taken them off to get a better view.

"I don't need special," I said quickly. "I just need you to come back another time, please."

"But I have flowers for you," he hollered, which really wasn't necessary, given that we were only metres apart.

"That's lovely, thank you, but you can leave them at the front door and I'll get them when I'm less...tied up."

"Phwoar, you're being a bit saucy, Miss Taylor."

For some reason, him using my real name gave me pause. He could have seen it in the papers or whatever, but he was being a bit personal, wasn't he?

"I'm not being saucy," I said. "You're the one turning everything I say into something...something rude."

I wanted to get out of his line of vision. My backside was stinging and must have been a state and a half, considering how much it hurt. I doubted I'd be able to sit on it for over a week.

"And I have an invitation for you," he babbled on. "To the party after the awards."

"I already have one, thanks but if you insist I have yours pop it through the letterbox if you don't mind and I'll get it in a second. As you can see, I'm in a bit of a delicate position."

His eyes disappeared. The letterbox flap clattered shut. His silhouette on the other side of the glass appeared as he stood upright, stubby and short and so very Johnny Bravo. Yet he didn't seem as short as usual. Maybe he'd perfected the art of making his quiff stand higher. After pausing for a second or two, he walked away.

Relief made my legs shake. I stayed where I was for a while so I was sure he'd really gone. Then I managed to roll over onto my side, grab hold of the newel post, and haul myself to my feet. Another set of hops got me to the kitchen, and I cut the knickers off with a pair of scissors.

I was so cross, and so sore, that I could have kicked myself for buying the wrong bloody size.

Feel a million dollars, my screaming arse.

5

The Boob Tape seemed to have vanished on me. I'd searched everywhere, but the delightful little roll of wonder tape couldn't be found. Roo-Roo was doing his usual, flapping around my house in a frantic effort to find it, and I started to panic.

If I couldn't wear the sheath dress, what *would* I wear?

I couldn't choose anything from my wardrobe that I'd worn before. The press loved to pick up on things like that. *Lola wears same dress as last month!* I had other dresses, ones that were bought for this kind of situation, but none of them were suitable for the music awards. I *had* to wear the black dress.

Roo-Roo came into my bedroom. Even though the towelling on my dressing gown was soft, it still chafed my backside every time I moved.

"Darling, we're doomed," he said, raising the back of his hand to his forehead. "Sellotape?"

"Tried that before, remember. It doesn't stay sticky for long enough." But his fabulous suggestion gave me another idea. "Hang on a second," I said, leaving the room.

In the garage, I ferreted about in a drawer where I kept odds and ends. I knew that what I was searching for was there because I'd used it recently to hem a pair of trousers. I couldn't sew and, well, I was creative in how I fixed things.

Ah, there it was, my silver saviour.

I took it back upstairs. Roo-Roo gave me the kind of look that suggested I was either crazy or I'd solved the world's problems. I waited to see which it was.

"You, my dear, are a genius." He strode over to me, kissed my cheeks, then stepped back. "You're going to need help putting it on."

I'd known that, and with any other man I'd have been uncomfortable, but not with Roo-Roo. I turned away from him to slip on a pair of sweat pants then took off my dressing gown.

I faced him again "Okay, we'll do a practise run. Shall I hold them up while you tape, or do you want to do it the other way around?"

A year ago, I never would have thought I'd be standing in front of a gay man, waiting for him to tape up my boobs.

"You hold," he said, "and we'll make them look Polly Perky."

So there I was, standing in my bedroom, cupping my assets while my best friend turned each of them into Polly. While he worked his magic, I wondered whether other famous women were doing this right now, but with The Boob Tape. It never failed to amaze me how some aspects of 'normal' life remained in 'famous' life—how getting ready for a party was sometimes fraught with dilemmas. What had I expected, then? For absolutely everything to change? I'd always had the philosophy that everyone was the same. No matter how much money they had or how high a status they had, everyone did similar things. I was oddly relieved that that was true. I'd been worrying that I was losing Charlotte, losing *real life*, that I had to *become* Lola—eat, sleep and breathe Lola—and all along, little pieces of Charlotte were still there.

I had to work out how to retain a balance, though. How to switch from one personality to another. The problem was, as I still didn't know who Lola should be and how she should act, I was a bit lost, even after a year in the biz. My being Charlotte when I'd first joined Celebland hadn't worked. I'd quickly realised I should act a certain way in order for them to accept me. I'd tried — and failed — loads of times, but I was a trooper and would soldier on.

Maybe if I made a proper, conscious effort to be like everyone else in this little bubble that being famous had put me in, I wouldn't have this dilemma.

"I'm going to try really hard to fit in tonight," I said, letting go of my boobs to see what effect the tape had on them. They didn't move. They were indeed Polly Perky again. The tape kind of pinched my skin, but it was a necessary evil.

Roo-Roo moved back to inspect his handiwork. "They're level. Phew! And they look *gorgeous*, darling."

"Should I use the tape to stop me having a muffin?" I stared at the roll in his hands, gauging whether there was enough left.

He reared his head back, widened his eyes and dropped his mouth open. "What kind of suggestion is *that*? You think you're *fat*?" He shook his head, horrified. "There isn't one item from a bakery on your body, petal, not one. Put the dress on, let me prove it to you."

I ushered him out of the room while I switched my sweat pants for sexy little knickers and the dress. I had a healthy cleavage and the muffin wasn't in evidence.

Roo-Roo came back in, offered me an I-told-you-so expression, then flopped onto my bed.

"Beautiful," he said, propping his head up with his cheek in his hand. "Not a Dunkin' Donut or a lardy cake in sight. So, tell me about this 'fitting in' thing."

As I took the dress off again, I explained how I'd felt when I'd first come into the limelight.

"Do what I do, dear," he said. "I'm one person with everyone else and myself with me."

I frowned. "So you're not yourself with me?"

He sighed. He seemed to be staring at nothing, seeing something in his head and thinking on what to say next.

"Petal, no one can truly be themselves with anyone *but* themselves. The only time I think there's an exception is when you meet your soul mate. I'd say you come extremely close to being able to be who you really are then."

He sounded sad, as though he wanted to find *his* soul mate.

I understood how he felt.

I draped the dress on a hanger then hooked it over the top of my bedroom door, so pleased I'd get to wear it later. Sitting on the bed, I wondered whether we were both at stages in our lives where we were lost.

"You'll find someone," I said, praying with all my heart that was true.

Roo-Roo deserved happiness. He was such a giving person, so nice and friendly. And he'd been a tower of strength for me. I had no idea what I'd have done without him, how I would have got through half the stuff I had. He'd been my mentor as I'd eased into stardom, and I'd met so many fabulous people while at parties with him.

"I don't know how," he said. "The kind of people who I'd want to have a relationship with wouldn't want one with me."

"Why not?" I frowned harder, staring down at my recent nail job—cerise pink polish and silver sparkles.

"Because they think I'm someone else." He smiled, the bittersweet kind that showed he might well be unhappy inside and was acting out a constant pantomime day after day. "And you, my dear darling, have the same problem, don't you?"

I nodded. "I want someone to love me for me, not who they think I am. But because of who they think I am, I'm never going to find him." I thought of my dream man and how he only lived in my imagination. I wasn't *that* naïve—I knew perfect men didn't really exist. But it wouldn't stop me hoping that at least an eighty per cent perfect one would come my way.

"Exactly, darling. So basically, with how Celebland is, how superficial a few of them are, we're both fucked!" He launched one of his deep laughs at me and bounded off the bed. "So, how are you having your hair, and when is the lovely stylist coming? I assume you're having the wonderful Chantelle over to do it?"

"Yes." I glanced at the clock on the bedside cabinet. "She'll be here in ten minutes."

"Ten minutes! You need to be in the shower right this second." He waggled a pointed finger at me before flouncing into the en suite. The shower splashed on. "Come along. In you get. I'll go and make you a nice cup of tea and let Chantelle in for you. There really isn't that much time left before we have to leave. Oh, and get that tape off. I'll sort your boobs out again once you're dry." He came back into the bedroom. "There's a fresh towel on top of the vanity, and I noticed your loofah's getting a bit tatty—must get a new one."

I cringed at the thought of the loofah touching my sore bum.

"So get a move on. This isn't any ordinary party night. There's a nice shiny award waiting with your name on it, petal. And you get to sing."

He winked then left the room.

In the shower—oh my God, the water stung my raw backside—I thought about how me and Roo-Roo were so similar. Maybe that's why we'd become such firm friends. Things in common, emotional things. Baggage, longings, dreams.

Dreams...

I had ten minutes before the stylist came. I smiled as I shampooed my hair. Was that enough time to think about Mr Perfect? I remembered where we'd got to last time, at Johnny's party. I'd left us in the foyer, him asking me if I'd brought a coat and me replying breathlessly that I hadn't.

I closed my eyes, massaged my hair, and allowed myself an escape.

"Then you must wear my jacket," he says. "I refuse to let my lady go out into the cold without some form of protection."

His voice is deep, mesmerising, and he's all gallant and whatever, and I decide to let him be whoever my subconscious wants. So what if he doesn't talk like the men of the East End or the movers and shakers, the stars. He's my own little bit of happiness, my dream man, and I could quite honestly fall in love with him.

"Thank you," I say.

He takes his jacket off then places it around my shoulders. It smells of him — lovely man musk and a hint of aftershave. The material is warm from his body, and for a second I imagine it's him draped over my shoulders and not the jacket. I feel protected, swaddled, and when he touches my face I can almost believe we're alone.

I look at him, wondering what he sees when he stares back at me. What I see are cloudy-day eyes, where they aren't quite blue and they aren't quite grey. I see faint smile lines around them, where he must have laughed a lot. I love a man who can make me laugh, and I hope, after he's had his way with me, he'll send me into fits of giggles. His mouth – God, I love it – is plump enough that I know his proper kisses will make my knees knock and my belly roll over.

What I see is the perfect package for many women. A gentleman.

"I could honestly lose myself in your eyes, Charlotte," he says, stroking my cheek with the back of his finger.

The same as when I'd met up with the hot man of my dreams before, I don't want to reply. I know the reason for that too. The real Charlotte has a habit of messing things up, of speaking before thinking, then being mortified afterwards. Lola does it too. So here, in my daydreams, I want to ensure I don't make any mistakes.

So instead of speaking, I sigh as an answer. He doesn't seem to mind. As we stare at each other, it's as though we're completely alone.

It's just me and him.

"So, to my boat on the Thames?" he asks.

I nod.

He takes my elbow and steers me out of Johnny Bravo's house, away from the madness inside it. We run down the driveway to his car – oh, it is a sporty little red number – and he opens the door for me to get inside. He leans in to help pull my seatbelt across, and his hand brushing mine has goosebumps sprouting up all over me. He secures the belt. Looks at me, his mouth as close as it can be without his lips touching mine.

Oh my days, he's going to kiss me. He's going to give me a proper kiss!

I hold back a squeal of excitement, breath catching in my throat. Close my eyes. Wait. Feel his breath on my skin. Hear his ragged breathing. Pucker my lips and –

"Will you get out of that *shower*, darling?" Roo-Roo called. "Really, you've been in there *ages*. What have you been doing, having a Herbal Essences moment?"

I might have been if you hadn't interrupted. "No! Almost done…"

I could only wish I was. There was so much more to do with my fantasy man. It was just a shame our secret liaison had been interrupted.

Again.

The red carpet was a splash of brightness, as were the flashes of cameras and the brilliant smiles of the celebrities. I nervously waited my turn to walk on it, hoping I didn't trip from catching my dress hem with my shoe heel. I didn't have Roo-Roo beside me for courage, but hey, I had David, and even if I were alone, I could do this by myself. I was much stronger than the woman who had first entered Celebland. I'd see Roo-Roo inside once I'd posed for the press and the many fans crammed together behind security barriers.

As a well-known rapper got out of his car, *the* rapper of the moment, the crowd cheered, women screamed and some poor girl fainted. He smiled for the cameras, winked a lot every time he lifted his shades, and generally played to the audience. He was due to follow me into the venue, but by the looks of things, he'd push in and go before me. He was edging his way closer to the end of the walkway, where a boy band had just done their bit, leaving the way clear for my entrance.

"Off we go," David said, taking my elbow. "He isn't the only star around here, much as he'd like to think so."

I stepped forward, nerves rattling a little, and smiled so hard my cheeks hurt. Shouts of "Lola! Lola!" had me turning every which way so that people could take pictures. I didn't want to let anyone down, and the fans had waited so long for their idols to turn up. It had been raining earlier, and some of them still had damp hair.

As I took another step, the rapper moved in front of us, side-on. He waved, smiled, showing off his new gold grills. They suited him, I had to admit, and he was a good-looking man.

I privately called him Twenny Pee.

"Excuse me," David said to him quietly. "Ladies first."

It was a gentle prod, but knowing David as I did, anger was brewing beneath the surface. He didn't like me being treated unfairly and fought to get me every job and as much into the limelight as possible. He took care of me in a fatherly way, and although he came off as stern sometimes, everything he did for my career was in my best interests.

He didn't have to have an altercation with Twenny Pee on my behalf, though. The rapper had a habit of writing about people who had upset him, creating lines in his hit songs that would be a forever reminder of any spats he'd had. He also had a custom of rapping instead of speaking, so if any argument was about to erupt, Twenny Pee would probably win it. He had a quick mind, and I'd heard he'd come into stardom after winning some kind of rap battle competition.

Twenny Pee turned to face us. I couldn't see his eyes behind his sunglasses to judge what mood he was in, but his smile vanished as he stared at David.

He rolled his shoulders. "They want me, innit, that much is clear. If you let me go first, I'll buy you a beer."

I held back a choke of laughter. I knew I wanted a man who could make me laugh, but not in this way. His everyday, in-normal-conversation raps were bad, but

Roo-Roo said no one would tell him in case they got immortalised in one of his records.

"I don't need a beer, thank you," David said crisply. "But *you* need some manners. It's Lola's turn next. Please move out of the way."

Twenny lifted his sunglasses. He perched them on top of his bald head, then narrowed his eyes — *this can't be good* — and puffed out his chest.

"I'll obey you for Lola, for nobody but her, but if you diss me again, I'll be taking my turn," Twenny rapped. "You diggin' me?"

David sighed. Rolled his eyes. "Yes, I'm digging you, but please…"

The press were taking pictures, and if they'd have been close enough to hear what had been said, it could have been made into such a big news item that we'd fill columns of the celeb pages for a week.

Twenny looked me up and down. Was he admiring me? Or was my duct tape showing somehow? He stared directly at my face after his slow-motion study and exposed his grills again.

Up close they were sparkling.

"Hey, little sugar, I think you're mighty fine. I think that by the end of the night, you're going to be mine."

This time I didn't want to laugh. He watched me so intently, instinct was screaming that he was being serious. Twenny Pee was interested in *me*? Like *that*? I wasn't sure how I felt about it. I found him attractive, no doubt about it, but surely he didn't…

So I smiled instead of answering. David sighed again then led me around Twenny before I had the chance to hear another rap. My dress scratched over my sore bum. But Twenny and my backside were soon forgotten as my role as Lola took over. Euphoria crested inside me as I did what I'd always dreamed of doing — being close to fans. I posed for the camera. Waved. Signed a few soggy notebooks and CD cases spotted with rain, an aide holding an umbrella over us. We walked along, pausing every so often, then we were inside the building. More red carpet. More press. I stood in front of a partition wall that had advertising on it and smiled yet again, amazed and excited that I was even there at all. Everything zoomed by in a blur, and by the time we reached the main arena, I couldn't remember much of my red-carpet walk.

The awards setting was done out like a massive restaurant. The main lights were muted, and old-fashioned, Victorian brass lamps attached to the walls gave a little more light around the edges. Candles in glass bowls flickered, their flame shadows dancing on the tablecloth. There were hundreds of tables, and oh my God, I'd never been anywhere like it before. It was amazing.

The stage at the back seemed so big, the royal blue curtains hanging with perfect pleats. I stared about in awe, for a second getting a pinch-me moment, where I thought I had to be in one of my daydreams — that the whole Lola thing was in fact a daydream, and I'd wake up in a minute, back in my old life.

I couldn't wait to get up there and sing.

David took us over to a drinks area. The bar was more like a buffet table covered in dark blue cloth that pooled on the carpet. Rows of champagne glasses were filled to just below the brims. Five men in tuxedos worked behind the table, shaking cocktails to order or pouring draft beer into pint glasses. The constant chatter sounded like a stream of white noise as I tried to come to terms with the fact that I was really here.

"Lola, darling!"

Rupert steamed towards me, weaving between tables, having got in via the pre-arranged side entrance as one of my table guests. Seeing him in his tailored suit coupled with a white shirt, was all that was needed to make my happiness complete. He reached me just as David handed me a glass of champagne and he gave me a kiss on the cheek.

"Those eyelashes won't come off if you encounter any hot air tonight, dear," Roo-Roo said. "I just about Superglued them on. So, how was the red carpet?"

I moved away from David, who was having a conversation with someone or other. I jerked my head a bit so Roo-Roo followed me. We stood against the wall the bar was on to give ourselves some privacy. I was conscious Twenny Pee might walk in any second and I needed to let Roo-Roo know what had happened.

"I think Twenny Pee is…um…thinking he might see me later," I whispered close to his ear.

He cocked his head and frowned. "Twenny Pee?"

I'd forgotten that Roo-Roo didn't always know the names I had for people. "You know, *the* rapper." I glanced around to make sure no one was within earshot. "Him."

"Oh my God. *Him?*"

"Yes, *him*," I said.

"Tell Roo-Roo all about it."

I whispered everything to him in a mad rush. My words tumbled out, not making sense. My face grew hot—talk about embarrassing—and Roo-Roo flapped his hand in front of my face to cool me down.

"Stop getting flustered," he said. "Your foundation will melt off."

I finished talking then asked, "Well?"

"Do you like him?"

"Yes, but..."

"So have a dabble." Roo-Roo smiled. "It wouldn't hurt. And if it gets out, having your name twinned with his isn't really so bad, not from a music perspective. Duets... He pulls in the crowds."

"He *raps* everything."

Roo-Roo shrugged. "We're all quirky in some way, darling. And besides, if you just fancied a bit of *company*, what does it matter whether he raps or speaks, catch my drift?"

Yeah, I caught it. But I didn't usually just sleep with people because I wanted to have sex.

Charlotte doesn't, but what about Lola?

"Look, wait until later," Roo-Roo advised. "Champers will help you to decide. For now, we have a wonderful dinner to eat then the awards ceremony. Then the party. The night is still young and we have oodles of time to worry about where you're sleeping."

I remembered something. "I can't sleep with anyone tonight. Not anyone."

"Why ever not?"

"The tape...?"

Rupert grinned. "I see. Well, I can take it off for you. Or you could do it yourself, surely. Just a quick rip— won't hurt a bit. Well, maybe a bit..."

"But my *bum*," I said, shifting my eyes left to right as people walked past. "The sheets will rub it."

"So sit on him then." Roo-Roo swatted the air. "Use your imagination, darling. It isn't all about the bed, you know."

He roared with laughter at that. I smiled then turned and saw Twenny Pee standing behind me.

"You have a mighty fine ass, sweet, sweet baby. So mighty fine that I need you as my lady." He took his sunglasses off, before popping them into his suit pocket.

He had pretty eyes for a man. And I did like him, despite his raps.

Before I could answer him, Deborah swanned in. She was alone and I remembered what had apparently happened between her and the footballer after Johnny's party. An anonymous lady had written in to a women's magazine and accused him of taking her to bed then dropping her off in the middle of nowhere at four in the morning. He'd been demoted to the sub's bench because of an injury, but there were rumours it was to keep him out of the limelight for a bit, until everything had calmed down.

"Hello, gorgeous," she said to Twenny, batting her eyelashes and taking possession of his arm. She gazed up at him as if he were a god.

Roo-Roo nudged me. I knew why. He loved watching her antics playing out. He said it was better than going to the cinema.

"Yo, lady," Twenny said in a rare moment of non-rapness. He gave her a filthy look then stared at me.

I smiled and shrugged, feeling awkward and 'in the middle of something', like I shouldn't be there now she'd turned up.

Deborah glared from him to me then back again. "I detect a slight...'thing' going on here?" she said.

"No, no. No 'thing'," I said quickly. *And if there is, I don't want you to know about it.* If I really, *really* liked Twenny and she knew it, she might spend all evening trying to lure him away from me.

"Riiiight," she said, keeping hold of his arm. She frowned at me then, and leant forward, scrunching her eyes up a bit. She smiled. Tossed her hair back over her shoulders by shaking her head. "Is that *duct* tape you've got holding your tits up, darling?" she shouted.

Ground? Hello, my names are Lola and Charlotte. Pleased to meet you. Can you open up right about now and swallow me? Kthnxbye.

"Remember, no flusters," Roo-Roo hissed.

But it was too late. My cheeks were hot again, and the more people stared at me, the hotter they got. Deborah had a smirk on her face. I felt like the kid in the playground with the bully. I felt like the geek beside the prom queen.

And you're just going to stand there like a wet blanket and take this kind of thing from her?

I opened my mouth to say something but Roo-Roo gave me a warning nudge to stay quiet.

"I cannot belieeeeve you," Roo-Roo said to her, but extra loud so those watching could hear. "You haven't got the latest Tit Tape? You haven't even *heard* about the latest Tit Tape? My God, lady, you need to get up to date a bit faster. You are *so* last week!" He swirled to face away from her, stuck his backside out, then looked over his shoulder. "And you see this? My cute little arse? You need to kiss it if you want me to keep my mouth shut about our makeup sessions, you hear what I'm saying?"

She kept her poise but I could see how Roo-Roo's comments had hurt her. I felt sorry for her. She gave us all a really weird look, one by one, as though she knew something we didn't, then walked away as if nothing horrible had happened at all. Twenny Pee seemed speechless for once, and I guessed he was already making up a few lines in his head for a future song.

"And you," Roo-Roo said to Twenny. "What kind of man lets a lady he's interested in be spoken to by a woman like that? Pray tell me, dear, for one would really like to know."

"It went too fast for me to do something about it, man, but if I have my way, that bitch'll be slummin'."

Roo-Roo chuckled. "That's what I wanted to hear. Now, darlings, it looks like we need to go to dinner. All the waitresses are converging on everyone. I'm glad, because my stomach feels like my throat's been cut. Chop chop!"

I went with him, pleased we were seated to the far right in a darkish corner. While we ate, I'd be able to think in between small talk, and I knew exactly what I'd be thinking about. Twenny using the word slummin' had stirred up a memory.

Funny how a word could zip you right back to the past.

I was about eight. Me and Jenna – four years older than me – had gone to the corner shop for some milk. Dad had said we could buy some sweets with the change, so we'd raced down there on Jenna's bike, her pedalling while standing up, me sitting on the saddle. I was so happy when I was with her.

It was hot, the sun was shining and, bearing in mind that Dad was dying for a cuppa, we had to get there and back quick. Dad worked long hours, so his first cuppa once he got home from work was always the best, he said. I usually made it for him, because I loved the big smile he gave me as I handed it over. That tea was probably the worst cup he drank every day, seeing as I was only young and didn't have brewing down to a fine art.

He was good like that, though, making out it was the best. He always made me feel good about myself and the things I did. He was the same with Jenna. God, we were so lucky to have him.

At the shop, Jenna didn't bother chaining her bike up – we couldn't afford a lock anyway – so she propped it against the wall before we went inside. We got the milk – only a pint – picked our sweets – a cherry lollipop for Jenna, a sachet of orange space dust for me – then strolled back outside.

Some kids were out there, boys, a crowd of them, messing about on Jenna's precious bike. It was too small for her – she'd had it given to her second hand from some woman down the road from our house – but we didn't care. Jenna, being the one who always said things how she saw them, stomped over and told them to, "Get off, you pigs." If Dad had heard that, she'd have been in trouble, but he wasn't there so that was okay.

Anyway, they wouldn't get off the bike. Said things to us like "You're nothing but a scab bag" and "You're so poor you even have to share a bike". We didn't mind sharing – we always shared – and God, we were grateful to have one bike let alone wishing we had two.

First, they threw the bike at us. One of the pedals scraped Jenna's shin, making it bleed. She didn't cry, though, just stared at them, clenching her fists. They snatched the milk off me and poured it out onto the pavement. I stared at the puddle as it spread and grew, some of it trickling over the kerb and landing in the gutter. Now Dad wouldn't have his cuppa, because he'd already said that was his last pound until payday, two days away.

They told her she was a dirty cow and she'd never ever ever have anything nice because she would never ever ever have any money.

"You're just slummin' it, you are. Always have and always will."

On the ride home, the air on my face dried my tears.

On the ride home, Jenna worried about the milk and Dad not having his tea.

And on the ride home, I promised myself that I'd do everything I could so our Dad never ran out of milk and my Jenna would have nice things.

I promised myself I would achieve that, no matter who bullied me.

I didn't win an award. My acceptance speech remained in my bag, precisely folded, the way it would stay until the day I was lucky enough to be nominated for something else. The Bombastics took the newcomer's prize, and I was genuinely happy for them. How could I be anything else? They were so pleased that they cried.

But there was no time to dwell on anything now. It was my turn to sing. I stood in the wings, waiting for my cue. Nerves always got to me at times like this, but I settled them a bit by telling myself that once I was out on stage, once I sang the first note, I'd be fine. Singing was what I'd been born to do, and hearing everyone clapping and cheering afterwards was such a buzz.

The presenter said, "And now, the woman you've all been waiting for. The incredibly talented Lola!"

Goosebumps rushed all over my body. My stomach seemed to turn over. The roots of my hair felt like they wavered, and I took in a deep breath. I released it, smiled brightly, then stepped out onto the stage. When I was at the centre spot, I made eye contact with those at the tables nearest the stage then searched for Roo-Roo and David, who were beaming and looked so proud of me I could have cried.

The music of my latest single started, an acoustic introduction instead of the original version, and although my voice wouldn't have the backdrop of the many instruments it would usually have, I was pleased to be able to have the chance to show the crowd and those at home watching on TV that I didn't need much music in order to sing.

As the show was live, I needed to give it my very best shot.

I thought of my busking days as the time for me to start singing drew closer. Pulled all those past emotions inside me, drawing on them for courage. My mouth was dry and I swallowed, reminding myself that David had seen something in me the day he'd spotted me on the platform. That I could give the crowd what they expected—a showcase of my vocal range and how much my voice had matured since last year.

The first line came out softly, as I'd intended, as did the rest of the first verse. I wanted to build up the strength, giving them a wow moment when the song reached a crescendo. My nerves melted away and the joy of singing took over. I was in my special place, the place where I was most comfortable, and I didn't want the set to end. I could sing all night.

The music stopped for a few beats between the second verse and the final chorus and closing lines. I held my breath, looking out at the crowd, sensing that they held their collective breath too. Another surge of goosebumps came, then I belted out the lines with force, holding one note and praying I could sustain it for the length of time needed.

The crowd went wild. People clapped and whooped, stood up and stared, some shaking their heads, others nodding.

I couldn't believe it—after numerous performances, I still couldn't believe I touched them the way I did.

Giving it my all, I sang harder, pushing out the high notes, the music fading to nothing as I finished the last lines of the song without accompaniment. It was silent save for my voice, and the air prickled with expectancy. On the last word, I strung it out as long as I could then bowed my head.

The feeling inside me was immense, a wave of emotion that threatened to have me crying. I'd hit every note just right and felt I'd given my best performance yet. I breathed heavily, trying to get my senses in order, trying to calm down.

The silence seemed to stretch on for too long.

Then the crowd erupted, swallowing that silence, a great wash of sound—clapping, cheering, whoops and screams. I looked up, seeing everyone on their feet, Roo-Roo doing a mad dance, gripping David's arm and yanking on it madly. David winked at me, his smile so wide it brought tears to my eyes. He nodded, and I knew I'd 'nailed it' as he would have said.

The presenter came over and hugged me. "Wow, Lola. You really gave it to us this time."

I smiled, my mouth still too dry for me to be able to say anything right that second.

"So, what's next for you?" he asked.

"I'm having a short break then I'll be promoting my new album in a couple of months," I managed, then licked my lips. I needed a drink of water so badly!

"You hear that, folks? You can get the album in your hot little hands very soon. Let's give it up for the fabulous Lola!"

I smiled and waved, filled with the bubbles of excitement I always got after singing. I left the stage, wishing I could go back out there and entertain them some more. Someone handed me a bottle of water, and I drank deeply then smiled to myself.

Nothing could beat that feeling of being on stage.

Nothing.

* * * *

I threw myself into the after-party, mingling like Roo-Roo did, laughing and generally having a good time. Tonight led me to sitting at a table with a couple of other female singers from a girl band while Roo-Roo romped off in search of future faces he could slather makeup on. He was always working, seeking the next opportunity.

The girls from the band had always been nice to me, seemed well able to handle the trials and tribulations of fame, so maybe I'd learn a thing or two from them. So far, I'd gathered that to get noticed more, to get better side jobs, their best advice was to sex my way to the top—to do the rudies with men who could further my career. That wasn't me—my imaginary lover was my ideal and I didn't think I could toss that dream aside as easily as those two women had—but I nodded and agreed with them anyway.

Cora, the blonde one, was on her fifth glass of wine. In the low lighting, she appeared mysterious and altogether in control of who she was. I wanted to ask her if she'd always been that way or if she'd had to learn how to behave in the world of celebrity.

Vixen, the brunette, was a different matter. I couldn't quite take to her. She'd confessed, after gulping down red wine, that she'd got rid of everyone in her pre-fame past and pleased no one but herself these days.

"She's a bit of a bitch, aren't you, Vixen?" Cora said.

"A bit? I'm a huge bitch." Vixen laughed.

"So, who are you shagging tonight?" Vixen asked me. "I see the rapper has his eyes on you."

She nodded, staring behind me, and I turned to see Twenny Pee talking to another rapper, their heads bent low, foreheads almost touching. Twenny was watching me in a way I thought was quite sweet, sort of how I might look at my dream man. I smiled at him — maybe it was the wine, maybe I'd just glimpsed a side of him he didn't show anyone else — but I could honestly see myself being at least friends with him.

I faced Cora and Vixen again. "He's probably looking at you two."

"Er, no." Cora shook her head then took a swallow of her drink. "I've tried it on with him and he wasn't interested. And so has Vixen, haven't you, Vix?"

"Mmm-hmm. Turned me down flat." Vixen leaned towards me. "I heard he's very selective. Doesn't sleep around like you might think. When he likes someone, he *likes* them."

I wasn't sure whether to be flattered or wary. It was all very well him liking me, and nice to know he wasn't a male tart, but I knew he wasn't my Mr Perfect, that he couldn't even come close, so what was the point in going with him?

"Look, just give him a go," Vixen said. "Have a sesh with him, see if he's any good in the sack. If he is, bonus, go back for more, but if he isn't…?" She shrugged. "Just call it an experience and move on."

I sipped more white wine. It had gone warm. "But…" How could I tell them what I really felt? That somewhere out there was my soul mate, waiting for me, and that I knew it, just bloody knew it? They'd possibly laugh me out of here.

"But what?" Vixen asked. "Listen, is it because you're well known that you don't want to risk a one-night stand?"

I didn't know.

"What would you be doing if you weren't one of us?" Cora asked. "Just say you're out now like a regular person, that we're not famous, and we're friends out on the lash. Don't tell me you wouldn't shag that man if you had enough wine in you." She lifted her glass in his direction. "Come on, when was the last time you *did it*?"

I didn't answer, but the look on my face must have given it away.

"There you go then." Cora smiled smugly. "Do it with him already. It's the right thing to do."

I drank another two glasses of wine while Cora and Vixen chattered on, telling me about the men they'd slept with and how it was obvious I'd never heard about it.

"See?" Vixen said. "So if you're worried about people finding out, they won't. Not if you or him don't tell anyone. And I heard he's the type to keep his business quiet, if you know what I mean. So if you go with him, you're safe from the gossip columns."

Could I trust these two? Or were they doing what The Snorters had, not giving me the whole story, setting me up for a fall?

Although I was enjoying the party atmosphere, I thought it might be best if I went home, so I thanked them for being so nice to me, said I was off to find Rupert, and left them to it.

I found him deep in conversation with Stella Randall, a singer he'd long wanted to work on—her face, that was. Seeing me, he said his goodbyes to her then all but dragged me to a private spot in one corner.

"What's the matter, darling?" he asked, taking hold of my hand and squeezing it.

"I'm confused," I said.

"Oh, aren't we all. Life is one big swirl of confusion. We just have to make the best of it, make sense of what we can and ignore the rest. What are you confused about?"

"Twenny Pee."

"Oh." He stuck his lips out. "If you're still thinking about it this late into the evening, it must be something you want to do."

"That's the thing. I think I want to, but only for...*company*." I was lying. That wasn't all. "And because... God, I can only ever admit this to you. I'm horny, okay? A girl needs some action once in a while and although I keep thinking it's wrong to want it, I still want it. Bloody hell, I'm not making any sense, am I?"

"Perfect sense," Roo-Roo said. "We all need a bit of *how's your father* every now and again. Pointless, mindless sex can be good for you. I understand why you're holding back, I really do — we both want our dream lovers, our forever partners — but sometimes you have to kiss a few frogs before you find him."

"It's more than kissing," I said, giggling.

"Okay, sometimes you have to share a bed with a few frogs. And so what? What does it matter whether you sleep around? What you do with your wotsit isn't anyone else's business but yours." He grunted. "And the person you're showing your wotsit to. Go and speak to him," Roo-Roo urged. "Go on. Look at him. He can't stop staring at you. And he hasn't let a drop of alcohol pass his lips all night — I've been watching him.

So you won't get beer breath in your face while you're doing the sexy business. Just give him a chance—and yourself. Let you hair down for once."

I trusted Rupert. And his judgement. If he thought it would be all right for me to have some company, and I'd been considering it all night anyway, then I was up for it.

I filled my glass with some wine from a bottle on a nearby table. Tossed it down my throat then looked at Rupert.

"See you later," he said. "Or not..."

I walked away from him.

Maybe Twenny Pee was my Mr Right—or my Mr Right for Tonight.

There was only one way to find out.

As I approached him, it was as though his friend knew what I wanted. He seemed to melt away into the crowd, which by now was blurry and loud. Everyone appeared to be drunk—what I could see of them anyway—and I fitted right in. There wasn't any press at the party, so we'd been told, so I could relax a bit with Twenny Pee, knowing I wasn't being watched as possible story fodder. But Deborah was around somewhere, someone who might drop a text to a reporter without batting an eyelid, so I still had to remain on my guard as best I could with a bottle of white wine sloshing around in my belly.

I don't do one-night stands. But I so want one!

I reached Twenny Pee and stood in front of him, searching my mind for something sassy to say. Something witty or funny. Something that would make him laugh so that he, in turn, would make me laugh.

He took my hand, lifted it to his lips and kissed it. Score for the gentleman factor. I'd never had anyone do that before, so it took a second or two for me to process it. He was undeniably hot, and I fancied him something rotten, and being with him was getting more appealing by the second.

Without saying a word, he led me to an empty, private booth. I sat beside him on a couch and stared out at everyone else rather than look at him. Charlotte was telling me that if I couldn't look at him, I wasn't doing the right thing. Lola was telling me that she'd like to have the balls to just go with a man for no reason and that it was the 'right thing to do'.

Twenny started rapping his latest single, the one about hoods and gangs, guns and fights, gorgeous women that he could *bleep* all night. His sensual, low voice made me feel hornier, but why was he singing to me? Why couldn't he talk?

"I like to count my money, sittin' by my honey. I like to buy her things, like gold and diamond rings." He stroked the back of my hand with his thumb, staring into my eyes. "I like to sit by the pool, and play with my big tool…"

Oh, God, he's changed the lyrics.

"And I'd like to sing or hum, while touching your peachy bum."

"Would you now," I said.

"My favourite show is ace, it gets mah juices flowin'. It isn't one about cops, or chefs or people sewin'. It's about this little lady, a woman just like youse, who enters my dreams and dances for me, wearin' nothing but her shoes."

Bloody hell! Was he saying he wanted me to do a striptease? I'd never done one before but…

"Maybe that could be arranged," I said, smiling.

"I'd take you on a flight, up to Heaven and back. I'd kiss your lips and touch your body, especially your sexy—"

Aaaaand that's enough of that.

I stood, ready to lead him from the party, but he tugged me down to sit beside him. He pulled me close, draped his arm around my back, and held me without saying a word.

We sat that way for a long time, not speaking. And so, when he got up and held his hand out, because he'd given me what I needed with that silent cuddle, I got up too and followed him out of the room.

Diary

It's a Rap

I can't believe I've had sex with Twenny Pee! :/

I woke up, thinking I was in my own bed, turned over, came face to face with the startling image of his golden grills. Niiiice! I could have sworn I saw my reflection in every one of those shiny teeth. I scared myself silly when I glanced in the bathroom mirror. My hair looked like I'd been dragged through a particularly thorny bush backwards, forwards, then backwards again. And my eyes! Pandas had nothing on me.

Last night I thought doing it with Twenny was the 'right thing to do'. Cora said it was, and I convinced myself she was right. Those few glasses of wine gave me more courage than usual, and all that chat from Cora and Vixen about sexing my way to the top had seemed such a great idea.

Bless him, Twenny's a lovely guy, but just not my kind of guy.

My God, though. What have I done?

OMG, he rapped at me *again*. "I want some more of your sexy titties, let me touch your groovy bitties."

In his sleep? He even rapped in his sleep!

I quickly got out of bed, scrabbling about in the semi-darkness for my clothes.

Luckily I found my phone and used the screen light as a torch. My knickers were hanging from the chandelier above the bed, and I had to climb onto the mattress, all the while praying he wouldn't wake up and think I was the adventurous kind who wanted to get into some kinky business.

I grabbed my knickers and found my dress—in a heap on the floor no less—and my shoes, each one propped on top of two different music awards he'd won.

Then I remembered the duct tape and wasn't sure if Twenny had seen it—whether I'd had the chance to take it off before we'd done anything. Talk about showing myself up.

I'm remembering waaaay too many details!

I remember running stark naked, making a mad dash through his penthouse to collect my bag and someone stepped in front of me.

I let out one of those silly squeals—the ones that make you feel ten years old again—and clutched my clothes to my body to cover my rudie-bits.

A woman was standing there, asking me if I was 'one of his women'. She was about fifty, looked foreign, and was wearing a white maid's apron.

And she knew who I was! I tried to make out that I was someone else, but I'm not convinced I fooled her to be honest.

I'm pretty sure that my 'little mistake' is going to be plastered all over the papers by tomorrow.

God, I'm blushing just thinking about it all!

I think this sums up my current situation. This part of my life?

It's a rap.

And yes, I know it isn't spelled right, but it means the same thing.

Origami 'Orridness

To fill the time between now and being able to go to the US for my holiday, I've been throwing myself into the party scene again. After the Twenny episode, you'd think I'd lay low, but no, not me.

Not Lola.

There was this one party where everyone was smoking weed and getting trashed. I just got drunk. Needed to try to get the Twenny thing out of my head. He got my number somehow, texted me to see if I wanted to 'hook up' with him again. I said no thanks—I feel awful, but I can't walk that road again. He's been nice about it, thank God. Sent me a little rap after.

One night with you, but I thought there'd be many, and what I don't get, is why you called me Twenny.

Could have died *on the spot*. I must have called his name out while I was err, you know. I should *not* do anything I'm uncomfortable with. I should listen to my own inner voice, not everyone else's. What's right for them isn't always best for me.

Anyway, enough of that. Back to this party. Vixen told me to have my hair done by this new stylist who's all the rage. She makes your hair look like *things*. You know, swans and roses or whatever. I thought it would be the 'right thing to do'— *again*. Everyone else seemed to be doing it.

She gave me origami hair! Some kind of pyramid made of triangles. Where was my swan, my bunch of flowers?

I went to the party like it. There were pictures taken. *Lots of them.* I smiled like a madwoman, thinking I'd finally done something the same as everyone else. The papers said otherwise. I'm a 'disaster area' apparently.

Jenna rang too, saying, 'What were you thinking?' in her usual blunt way.

That's the trouble. I wasn't thinking.

Sometimes going inside my head is more trouble than it's worth. In this situation, *not* going inside my head is more trouble than it's worth.

Confused again! Right-oh. Time to get a grip and move on.

☺ ← See? I'm happy. Big smiley face etc. etc., blah blah blah.

Sing Again

Sometimes the most random thoughts come into my head. I remember things and just have the urge to write them down. So here we go. More ramblings.

So I got to thinking of when I first met David. I was on the platform, right, and it was really busy and full with people waiting for trains or squeezing past others to get closer to the edge. I was at the back, squashed against the wall, because, you know, some people are just that rude. Anyway, I thought, I'd take the chance to sing now, while there was enough people around to hear me. I put my beret on the floor (just about enough room for it there) and started playing my guitar. A few commuters turned round to look but quickly turned back again.

I was just another busker. A nothing in their lives. And do you know what was funny? Well, not funny ha ha, but the other kind of funny? All I wanted to do was sing and give them a bit of happiness. Okay, that's not totally true.

I wanted to give myself a bit of happiness too because that's what singing does to me. Makes me happy.

I started singing, and it was like I was standing there silent. I might as well not have opened my mouth at all. No one, as far as I could see, turned around. But it didn't matter, I sang anyway.

So I closed my eyes, and even when the sound of a train coming drowned me out, I kept going. The shh of it arriving at the station, the breeze of air as it came to a stop, told me these people were going to carry on with their business while I carried on with mine. They'd get on the train, go to work, go home, whatever, and I'd still be there, waiting for the next rush of people to come along.

I heard the chink of coins being dropped, and I hoped it was in my beret and not someone losing their cash on the platform. I needed the money so I could buy milk, among other things. Even a couple of quid would have done it.

The shuffle of people moving en masse. The announcer's voice. The rude squeal of the train moving off. And suddenly I sensed someone actually listening. Standing in front of me and listening. I didn't open my eyes, just carried on, because I didn't want to be disappointed to see there was no one watching me after all.

But I can dream like the best of 'em, so I pretended there was and that my voice, the words I was singing, made a difference.

Another train came. Then the quiet. So I imagined I was on stage in a massive auditorium and that the echo of my voice was bouncing off beautifully decorated walls instead of dirty underground ones.

I ended the song. Opened my eyes.

A man was standing in front of me. He was in a suit, a dark grey one, and he was staring at me as if he was in shock. So, I stared back, my face getting hot because a) someone was actually there and b) I was wondering what to do now. Should I sing some more? Smile, pick up my beret, then walk away?

He asked my name.

I know London. Know it like the back of my hand. And I know what kind of people live here. He could have been Mr Weirdo disguised as Mr Business Man. He could have been Mr Husband disguised as Mr Pervert. He could have been anything at all. I just didn't know. But he looked kind—and I *know* that doesn't mean anything and he could still have been an oddball.

Except he didn't strike me as anything but a man asking a simple question.

So I told him my name.

He asked me if I sang there often, while he held his briefcase in one hand and rubbed his chin with the other. Of course at the time I was thinking his case could have a gun in it or rope to tie me up once he'd abducted me. It could also just have held a small laptop and a few pens.

We had a brief conversation about how often I was there, because he hadn't seen me there before, yada yada, and he asked me to sing another song for him.

To have someone ask me to sing a specific song... It'd never happened before.

So I sang—and sang and sang and sang.

I was a bit embarrassed by this point, standing there waiting for him to say it was a load of old crap, but he handed me his business card.

Anyway, I took it while he told me to make sure I called him because he wanted to hear me sing again. I wondered why he didn't just come back to the station and take a chance I might be there.

He walked off, not looking back, and I watched him, thinking that the whole thing was a bit surreal.

I remember staring at my beret. It only contained a pound coin, fifty pence and a few coppers. Oh, and a balled up tissue and what looked like used chewing gum.

Then I lifted the business card and read what was on it.

DAVID STONE. ARTIST MANAGER.

I seriously thought I was going to faint.

8

The Snorters were puking. We'd just been given lunch to *stop* us puking—from nerves—but off they went to say hello to it again in the toilets. God, I was standing there in the makeshift cafeteria scoffing a double cheeseburger and still reckoned I'd get into my size ten. When they'd seen what I was about to eat, they'd stared at me as if I had two heads, like I was the strange one. I felt so sorry for them that they'd been pressured into being so slim—that they were willing to do whatever it took to *remain* slim.

It wasn't just the trio I'd met in the loos at Johnny Bravo's party, either. Here, about twenty of them had legged it in a stampede, trying to beat each other to the ladies' room.

Bloody hell, those poor women…

While I waited, alone, for them all to come back, I thought about the dress I was expected to wear. I was going to feel like a mermaid, I knew it, because of the tight-fitted sequined body then the flare of taffeta at the bottom. I'd have to waddle, no doubt about it. But being a mermaid was something I'd never have been back in the old days, and it might turn out to be a big ball of fun.

The Snorters returned.

A man came in as well and called us from the doorway. "Come on, girlies, time to get pretty."

The Snorters seemed to drift to the door all at once, so I waited until they'd gone before I followed.

In the dressing room, I sat at my section while a hairdresser gave me another up-do of origami hair. I sat there for over an hour. Once she was done, I thanked her.

"We're not finished yet. That's just the first stage," she said.

"How much longer?" I asked.

"About another hour."

Oh my God…

I stared at my reflection in the mirror but failed to see it after a few seconds as my eyes had glazed over. I tuned out the chatter around me and decided to visit with my Mr Perfect.

It had been a while since I'd had the time to devote to him, but I hadn't forgotten the last time I'd seen him. I'd been in the shower the night of the duct tape, the night Twenny…

Don't think about that.

I couldn't exactly think about my dream man in a saucy way while someone was tugging at my hair, so I decided it might be better if we fast-forwarded through the rude bits and moved along to afterwards. Of course, it went without saying that the sex with him had been awesome, that he'd blown my mind and given me that Herbal Essences moment I'd been denied last time. I thought, too, that he would have made my legs go weak, that I hadn't been able to breathe properly, and that it was the best experience I'd ever had.

It couldn't be anything less.

When I met the man who could do that for real, I knew I would have found my soul mate.

After a shower with him, I let him dry me. He takes the time to compliment my expertise in the shower, making me feel that at last, I really have done 'the right thing'. He carries me to the bed in his big, strong arms and puts me down gently before he stretches out by my side. Then he folds me in a hug and strokes my wet hair and whispers lovely things.

"*Such a beautiful woman, Charlotte.*"

Bless his heart.

"*This has been the best day of my life, Charlotte.*"

And mine.

"*I want to spend the rest of my life just loving you, Charlotte.*"

Love me forever, you sexy, wonderful man.

"*Will you let me do that?*"

Let you? Of course I'll bloody let you.

My eyes droop. He sings a song – doesn't matter what it is, anything will do, even Any Old Iron *– and I smile and sigh and ooh and ahh at the sweet things he sings, then says. He tells me we'll have children – something I really want – and a dog – I want one of those too – and that we'll be happy forever and ever, amen. And I want* that *too.*

It seems we both want the same things. Funny, that.

"All done!" a woman said.

I blinked out of my daydream to find that I was still sitting in the chair. A bit taken aback by the transformation, it took me a moment to realise it was actually me. The stylist had given me mermaid hair that was so beautiful I wondered how she'd managed it. The waves she'd created now stuck out all over, held rigid, I assumed, with a can of hairspray for each hank. I had to admit, she was clever. I looked like I was in water. You know the way hair goes when you float on the surface? That was what she'd done.

"Wow," I said.

"You like it?"

"Yes, thank you."

"Great."

She walked away, her one-word answer still floating around inside my head. I thought I might have offended her. I wanted to go and find her, to let her know I really did love it, but the surprise of it had stopped me being able to say what was inside me.

But finding her wasn't going to be simple. The room was getting busier. By the time I'd done the runway stint, she might be gone. I had to go to the after-party as well—maybe she'd be there? David had said it was important that I mix with certain people and that it was better that I attend. For all I knew, one of the guests could book me for a private party. That would be nice, wouldn't it? I could pay off Jenna's mortgage with the money and buy Dad that little Fiat he'd had his eye on for ages. He hadn't allowed me to help him out to any grand degree, but I was determined that he would have the option to give up work if he wanted to. He was still plodding along, preferring to pay his bills himself. All I could do was surprise him with some shopping, clothes and things that could be classed as gifts.

And the milk. Whenever I visited him at his place, I always took him a pint of milk. I made him a cuppa too, wanting to see his smile as I gave it to him.

Old habits die hard. The wants of childhood still remained, even though I'd become an adult.

One of The Snorters screeched, pulling me out of my thoughts. I turned my head quickly to look to my right. An ultra-skinny blonde model had a red handprint on her very white cheek. A drop of blood was beading at the corner of her mouth, and I scooted my chair back in shock so I could get out of the way if the fight carried on. My heartbeat went crazy—I hated confrontation. I got out of my seat and made my way to the back of the room, feeling like an alien in a situation that was so foreign to me it had my eyes stinging.

Talk about being out of my depth.

Blonde Snorter shrieked again then launched herself towards a black-haired woman. They fought—oddly, they respected one another's hair-dos, which I found seriously surreal—until a tiny man in a tuxedo came in and trilled at them in a feminine voice that if they didn't stop it, they'd be fired.

They stopped.

I watched in awe as they continued getting ready for the show as if nothing had happened. Makeup artists appeared from nowhere and began applying the paint. I ventured to my chair, wondering what my artist would do to me. While she busied herself with creams and brushes and eyeshadows, I tried desperately to disappear back into my own little world. Okay, me and Mr Perfect were only sleeping in daydream land, but that was all right. I was in a happy place.

I wake beside Mr Studly and watch him while he sleeps. He has a hairy chest, which is just enough rough over smooth, hard pecs. I sift the fuzz through my fingers, loving how it tickles, and hold my breath in case what I'm doing wakes him up.

He doesn't stir — much — just sighs, which lifts then lowers my hand, as though it's a part of him.

I took that as a symbol my subconscious was telling me he was The One—or the kind of man waiting out there in real life for me. And it didn't need to tell me, I already knew. That I wanted to have a relationship with someone where it felt like I was literally a part of them and they a part of me. Like we were fused somehow, mentally and physically, where when one started a sentence, the other finished it. Where when I had a thought, he spoke it out loud.

Did such relationships even exist?

I'd read about them, but really? Truly?

I had to hope they did, because otherwise, one of my major dreams wasn't going to come true. And it wouldn't if I didn't find my real-life fantasy man.

I sighed.

"Oh dear," the makeup artist said. "I'll have to do that bit again now, love."

What bit?

Oh no. My sigh must have been the kind where my head had wobbled or something. Right at the point where she'd been applying eyeliner. I had a wiggly dark blue line going from the outside corner of my eye heading towards my cheek. All this poor woman's work was ruined. The end of her eye pencil was missing — it must have broken off.

"Oh, I'm so sorry," I said. "I wasn't paying attention."

"No worries," she said, using a wet wipe to get rid of the offending squiggle.

Thankfully, the artist finished pretty soon after that. I marvelled at what she'd created. My skin was covered in a light blue foundation that shimmered. My cheeks had drawn-on bubbles all over them. And my lips had been painted like those old-fashioned dolls.

I didn't look like me at *all*.

But you know what? It was nice to look like a mermaid.

9

Runways were deceptive. On TV there seemed to be enough room for two people to walk down them. I stood to the side of one that was surely only three inches wide. It narrowed even more the farther away it went.

How was I going to strut down it in my mermaid outfit?

"Get ready," the short man with the woman's voice said from behind me. "It's your turn next."

I swivelled to look at him and smiled.

"Remember," he said. "No looking at the crowd. It'll put you off. Scare you."

"Okay," I said, my voice reflecting my nerves.

Anxiety was doing a number on me again. I'd have thought that by now I'd have learnt how to control the nerves, but nooooooooo. My stomach cramped and I really wanted to go to the ladies' room.

"Small steps," he said kindly.

I stood in the wings—a corridor created from two stud walls, with electrical leads and clothes on hangers dangling off them. It was cold, probably owing to the high ceilings in the warehouse type thing the event was being held in, and my nipples had started to stand up.

"Nice pair you have there," he said, nodding at my boob area.

My dress was similar on the front to the ones that The Snorters had worn at Johnny's bash. A transparent turquoise panel went from the high neckline down the centre of my body and stopped just above my knickers.

Thank Heaven for small mercies. I glanced down at my chest. And yes, my nipples were definitely perking. They were currently trying to poke through the material like a couple of prison escapees.

"Um…thank you?" I said.

"You're welcome. I appreciate breasts very much. Don't get me wrong, I'm not a pervert, I just admire the female form for what it is. A piece of art. Now, back to business. Once Ella and Krystal come back, you're on the walk. See how they're turning at the bottom there? Without slipping or bumping into one another? There's an art to it."

"I don't know that art," I said. "No one's told me how I'm supposed to do this. I was told to turn up and that someone would give me some lessons, but no one did and I…" I stopped myself from rabbiting on.

He patted my arm. "No one expects you to do it perfectly, don't worry," he said, going up on tiptoe and leaning forward a bit to stare more closely at my prisoners.

From the corner of my eye I saw Ella and Krystal coming back up the walk and I needed to compose myself.

I hobbled closer to the stage, knowing that as soon as Ella's right foot hit the small red cross on the floor, I had to make my entrance. There it was, her wedge-heeled shoe on the cross, then she was breezing past me, rushing off to get changed into another amazing creation.

"Go, go, go, 'Normuss Nipples," the little man said, winking.

Laughing at his comment—he'd said it to put me at ease, I was sure—I stepped into the limelight, immediately looking at the crowd. Great, I'd gone and done exactly what he'd told me *not* to do. I couldn't help it, though. Normally, when I went out on stage I made a point of making eye contact with as many of the audience as I could. Men in suits, or jeans and T-shirts, sat with women in fancy dresses in row upon row either side of the runway—which still appeared to be three inches wide.

I smiled as everyone cheered and clapped, and I guessed they knew it was me, despite my crazy hair and makeup. They were holding pamphlets with my photograph on the front. Some of the women used them as fans.

I took my first step, and it was as if the dress had decided to turn into the shapewear knickers and squeeze any life out of my legs.

Come on, you can do this…

I walked like I'd had an accident in my underwear, quite frankly, but I pushed valiantly on, my chest tight and my heart beating like the clappers. I stopped looking at the crowd and navigated the narrow runway, feeling as though I was an elephant on a tightrope.

All I need is a colourful stripy ball…

My lapse in concentration meant one of my heels chose that moment to skid inwards. I wobbled, waited for the runway to kiss my bum, and was amazed when I was still upright. The crowd gasped—I suspected in anticipation of me going down—then *ahhed* as I continued down the walk. The shoes pinched my toes, the dress clung on even tighter, and I knew I wasn't going to make it back again with the heels on. At the end of the runway, I did my attempt at a flawless turn

but ballsed it up by skidding again. My ankle twisted —
God, that bloody hurts —and a nasty throb took up
residence in my Achilles.

I shrieked. And shrieked again.

In slow motion, I lurched sideways, heading to land
on the seated crowd, flinging one arm out as I cruised
down. Unfortunately, my hand made friends with an
old man's face, and he huffed out hot breath on my
wrist, poor fella. From wherever angels spring from,
two burly men appeared, whipping me back up onto
the stage. With a giddy head — and too many swear
words inside it to count — I had two choices. Walk back
up the runway in the shoes or do what I'd been warned
not to do — and take them off.

With a big smile cemented on my face, and as much
bravado as I could muster, I took them off.

I hung the back straps over two of my fingers, lifted
my arm and let the shoes dangle against my back. I
threw a cheeky grin at the crowd then began the walk.

It seemed their collective gasp would roll on forever.

I'd embarrassed myself, the other models, my
manager — everybody involved in this thing. Never
would I agree to model in this way again. Never. The
shame was too much. And the guilt over failing.

A woman cackled out laughter. I recognised it but
didn't dare to scan the crowd to see if I was right. The
last thing I needed at the moment was to set eyes on
Deborah. How did she always wangle herself an invite
to things like this? Why did people let her come when
they knew she was such a troublemaker? And why
would they risk being anywhere near her, or her being
able to see what they were doing, when she was only
famous, as far as I knew, for being a sexual predator
and selling tales?

Someone started a slow clap. Then another person joined in. As I somehow managed to sashay my bum and swing my hips, the clapping got quicker and wilder. By the time I landed on the red cross, the whole place was on their feet, cheering and shouting "Bravo!" and "Yes, break the mould!"

I'd very nearly broken my bloody leg, but I'd take breaking the mould, particularly if it meant I'd fixed the mistake I'd made.

"Lola!" the little nipple-loving man said as he came out onto the stage. "We have the delightful Lola!"

He didn't look angry at what I'd done—*go me for saving the day*—and he grasped my hand tightly as the crowd continued to display a wonderful amount of support.

I waved and smiled, curtseyed and bowed, then got myself off into the wings. I rushed to get my dress off then put on my own comfortable clothes. I felt slightly elated from the reaction of the crowd, and really quite proud of myself for turning a disaster on its head. I had to leave my hair and makeup as it was—for after-party purposes—but I really had the urge to wash my hands in the porta bathroom to get the sweat of a close call off my skin.

I stared at my reflection in a rust-spotted mirror propped up behind one of the taps in the loo and thought about what had just happened. I knew David did whatever he thought was best for my career, and although he said he was doing things for my own good, I needed to have a discussion with him about some of the jobs he put me forward for. There were things I'd prefer to decline—things I didn't want to do—and it was about time I said so. I was grateful to him for spotting me on the platform, but I had to be able to have a say in matters.

Taking control of my life was the way to go. Plus, The Big Apple was waiting for me with open arms. I had one more job to do after this one then I could go.

Someone barrelled into the bathroom. I couldn't work out who it was—she had makeup similar to mine—but she ran into one of the stalls. The sound of her being sick worried me, so I decided to check on her.

"Are you okay?" I asked.

"Yes," she said. "I must have eaten something that didn't agree with me."

At her insistence, I left her to it, feeling wicked for doing so but unable to think of how to help her.

I wandered out through the back door and into a private car park. With my crazy hair and my crazy face to keep me company, I sat on the concrete, my back against a wall and stared up at the moon. I was more confident now, happy because I'd turned a potentially bad situation into something good.

"Do you know what, Mr Moon? I'm going to The Big Apple soon. You have no idea how excited I am about that. And as for how I've been feeling lately… I knew what I was getting into with this fame thing—sort of, kind of. I wanted this. And I got it. I haven't been here that long compared to others, and I want to be around for quite a while, and I'm going to do my best to stay here."

It felt good to say it out loud.

"So," I said, "I'm going to get my head down and do my job. Then I'm going on holiday. I'll see you there."

If anyone was listening to me, they'd think I'd finally flipped my lid.

I went back inside to a full dressing room. The Snorters were either snorting lines, drinking Smirnoff Ice straight from the bottles, or gulping wine from plastic beakers. They argued, laughed, shouted and whispered. I said hi to them all and changed into my party dress.

I looked around and decided I was happy enough being me.

Life wasn't too bad at all!

10

Another party, another round of wonderful insanity. People seemed to be talking really fast, their actions quick and sharp, yet mine felt sluggish. They told me all their great ideas, as though I had a sign on my head that invited each guest to share their business with me. It was crazy, *so* nuts, and it took a while for me to get used to the pace. I caught up eventually.

The Snorters were well away, off their trolleys. I'd so far had a couple of glasses of white wine, but they were already churning in my stomach because all that was on offer was the fizzy kind.

I'd managed to get Roo-Roo a pass to the party. We stood together along a back wall. Roo-Roo hooted out laughter whenever the fancy took him, not caring if guests stared at us. He'd told me he wasn't bothered by what people thought of him, or whether they sold his gossip to the papers, because he was one of the best artists in the business and most of them wanted him to make their face up at one time or another.

"This party is fabulous, darling!" Roo-Roo said to one of the models, who he kissed on the cheeks. "Mwah, mwah!"

Roo-Roo seemed to have an effortless relationship with anyone who walked into the room. He had no problem starting conversations—even if it was meaningless jibberish, folks wanted to hear from him and talk to him as soon as he entered the party.

He was bold and outrageous, but nobody seemed to mind. He was a guaranteed table dancer by the end of the evening and there wasn't a champagne bottle unturned when Roo-Roo was around. Still, no matter how out of his face or embarrassing he was, everybody loved him.

He usually walked straight over to the most famous person at the party. He didn't wait to be spoken to—he strutted right up to them as if he owned the place.

I'm going to get me some of that magnetic pull on the 'in crowd'!

I supposed it helped that he was gay and he could follow the ladies into the toilet and touch up their makeup all night, but that couldn't just be it.

His cool persona and down-with-the-trend lingo definitely worked in his favour.

I could be as fun as him. I could go 'wild' and apply the 'YOLO' attitude to more areas of my life.

Sod it. I can also be the life and soul of the party like my best friend. My bestie is so cool.

Hashtag Proud.

"Would you just *look* at that *woman*!" he shouted to me above the thudding music once the model had walked away.

"Shh! You've had far too many drinks," I said, glancing about to make sure whatever woman he was referring to hadn't heard him. The music was pretty loud, though, so I thought he'd got away with it.

"I haven't had nearly enough, darling, if I'm going to be in this type of company all night. I mean," he said, jamming both hands on his hips, "this lot are more hyper than our usual crowd, don't you think?"

I had to agree with him. 'This lot' were letting it all hang out in a way I'd never seen before. Some of The Snorters were dancing with their boobs on display.

"What woman do you mean, anyway?" I said, thinking I knew already.

"Deborah, of course."

I nodded. I'd been right.

She was hanging off the shoulder of Nipple Lover— she had wickedly high heels on—and his eyes were level with her chest. It was a good job he enjoyed boobs as hers were spilling out of the top of her dress. She had some kind of pretty glitter on them, so every time she moved her skin sparkled in the light of the disco strobes.

"I wonder how much she paid for those," Roo-Roo said, touching one finger to his lips. "I think I might have to ask her one day."

"Don't," I said. "It might embarrass her."

"And I care because…?"

"Shh," I hissed. "She's coming over."

Her dress was some magnificent affair, all blazing red velvet with a diamond brooch on one shoulder. She swayed her hips as she walked the last few feet to us. Then she stopped directly in front of me and gave me a smile. I smiled back, keeping it sweet, and she dug into her handbag, all the while staring at me.

"Here," she said, holding out a roll of duct tape. "I saw your"—she gave my chest the once-over— "deflated balloons earlier so thought this would come in handy. The only thing even remotely solid about those things is the nipples."

"Oh," Roo-Roo said, snatching the tape from her. "This is just what I need. I have a hot date tonight with a man who loves it kinky, know what I mean?" He winked. "He likes being tied up, and this beautiful stuff gets slapped across his pouty little mouth on regular occasions."

"Oh, really!" Deborah said, clearly shocked and disgusted. Her mouth turned down and her nostrils flared. "Toooo much information, you filthy big oaf."

"I thought you liked filthy men," he retorted, staring past her to Nipple Lover.

She turned to see who he was looking at, then glared back at us. "Him? Good God, no."

"Oh. My mistake." Rupert smiled. "I did wonder whether even you had the balls to mess around with him. Selling his story would make sure you never set foot in a celebrity party again. So, have you finished trying — and failing — to torment my friend, or is there something else up your sneaky little sleeve? If there is, just get on with it so we can spend the rest of the evening without having to smell Eau de Bullshit."

She scrunched her eyes up in spite before she realised she'd showed him that he'd got to her.

"Yes, there was something, actually. How very perceptive of you." She reached into her bag again. "A little bird told me a secret. It twittered…"

I'd avoided all social media for a while. I hadn't been checking lately and now I wished I had. If someone had said something about me on there… No, David would have seen it and let me know.

"Did it now?" Roo-Roo pursed his lips. "And I'm sure you're going to tell us what it is, so come on, out with it. I'm feeling a little faint — that's how much it stinks in our vicinity." He squeezed his nostrils with finger and thumb then waved his hand in front of his face.

He was so rude, but I loved him to bits.

"You really are a little…" Deborah sighed. "No, I'm not going to allow you to annoy me." She took her hand out of her bag. "I thought you'd like this." She looked at me. "A reminder of where you came from and what you've become." She kept whatever was in her hand hidden. "When you think about it, you haven't really come that far at all. Your busker story was such a sweet little fairy tale I'm sure, where you earned mere pennies, and your love life is just the same, where you earn pennies yet again."

I had a sinking feeling in my tummy. "My life is none of your business," I said. "I don't understand why you keep trying to upset me."

"Because, my dear…" She leaned closer. "I. Just. Don't. Like. You."

She pressed something into my hand then walked away, glancing back over her shoulder, her trademark smirk splashed all over her face.

"Don't look at it. Give it to me," Roo-Roo said. "Whatever it is, you don't need to see it."

"But I do. I have to make sure I know what she's up to. If I don't, and this turns out to be one of her story-selling tricks, and I didn't warn David about it, he won't have a suitable response ready for the newspapers."

"True." Roo-Roo nodded. "Okay, so look at it. Quickly, darling. Just a little peek then throw it away."

I turned so my back was facing the direction Deborah had gone.

"It's all right, petal, she's with the nipple man again. Show me."

I lifted my hand and uncurled my fingers.

Saw a twenty pence piece.

"Oh, God…" I felt sick. "She knows!"

"How the hell does she? It's only me who knows you call him Twenny Pee, isn't it?"

I bit my bottom lip. "Um…"

"Oh, what have you done?"

I handed him the coin. It felt like it was burning my hand. "I...um... Oh, God."

"What? Hurry up and tell me before I get my knickers in a twist." Roo-Roo shuffled from foot to foot.

"I had a text off Twenny. After, you know..."

"And?"

"And he asked why I called him that." I closed my eyes so I didn't have to see Roo-Roo's reaction.

"Oh. Em. Gee. No. Really, no. You *didn't*!"

I opened my eyes. His were wider than I'd ever seen them, his mouth too.

"I must have." I covered my cheeks with my hands.

"You *must* have? What, you mean you don't *know*?" he wailed. "Oh, Lordy."

"Okay then, I called his name out." Shame was burning a hot path all over my face. The ground refused to swallow me up.

"What else do you remember, just in case we need to work out a story?" He rested his hand on my arm. Stroked it.

"I remember leaving the party. Then we went to his place. I know I dumped my bag on a table in his hallway, and after that we... Then I slept, waking up the next morning and that's about it."

"Why didn't you tell me this before?" He appeared mortally offended. "I mean, we share *everything*."

"I didn't want to admit I'd maybe been stupid. I'd had a lot of wine that night. And after...well, I didn't want to talk about it much because I couldn't believe I'd done it with him. I was horny, if you recall—and that's the only reason I had sex with him. I just wanted..." I paused. "I just wanted sex. Some kind of connection."

"Oh, darling..."

"Don't give me sympathy. Not here. I don't want her seeing she's achieved what she wanted. So we can't leave just yet."

"No, we can't. So we'll dance. We'll have fun like we always do. And she'll never know anything's wrong, all right?"

I nodded.

The next hour or so drifted by in a haze. I left the dance floor to get a bottle of water, leaving Roo-Roo to continue dancing away with some man or other. Deborah had left ten minutes earlier with another footballer so I was safe from bumping into her again tonight.

The water settled my tummy a bit, and I leaned against a wall to take a few deep breaths.

A footballer came up to me. I'd seen him on TV but I couldn't remember what team he played for. I think he wore a red football shirt on the field. He was good-looking—the current football star player—tall and toned, and when he asked me if I was all right and put his arm around me in a friendly gesture, I leaned into his side. We spoke for a little while about this and that. Nothing too deep, just stuff. It was nice just to be held, just to have someone other than Jenna or Roo-Roo who genuinely cared if I was upset or tired. A new friend. It was nicer that he didn't chat me up or say suggestive stuff.

It was nice, too, that I could take the comfort he offered without him expecting anything in return.

What a nice man!

11

Today was my last work day before I flew to America. It was a photo shoot for my upcoming album. While David knew what kind of feel he was after for the cover, he wanted to try various things in case his original idea didn't work out or look good. That meant me changing into loads of different outfits and having my hair styled in several ways.

These things could take all day, and by the time we were finished I knew I'd be knackered—but a good knackered where I felt lots of work had been accomplished. I had been tired after the shoot for the cover of my single, but it was all part of the job and I was happy to do it. I didn't like the feelings I sometimes got while being photographed, though. As I knew from my time on the runway, I was no model, so posing for pictures didn't come naturally. How they came out as well as they did, I'd never know. They didn't show my anxiety or whether I was uncomfortable in whatever pose I'd contorted myself into. They didn't show me thinking, *How am I even doing this?*

I sat beside David in the back seat of his car behind the tinted windows while we waited for some passers-by to…pass by. We were parked outside a hotel where the street was pretty busy and plenty of people might recognise me once I got out. Thankfully, no press appeared to be around—*no leaks, yes!*—so all we had to do was get me from car to hotel with the minimum amount of fuss.

"Right, let's go," David said.

He got out, scanned the street then gave me the nod. I joined him on the pavement and he ushered me inside the hotel. I had big sunglasses on—Black Fly Eyes as Roo-Roo called them—so at least I could hide behind those.

In the foyer, a man in chinos and a white T-shirt was flicking through a brochure while he sat on a leather sofa. A woman sat next to him doing the same, a little boy driving his toy train up her leg. I smiled to myself. They looked so happy, and I wondered whether I'd have the same thing they had someday.

I will, I know it. I just have to wait for us to meet, that's all.

And wouldn't that just put the icing on my cake of life? I'd have everything I'd ever wanted then—and I was so aware that not everyone did and that I was lucky. Not a day went by, even when I was tired, that I wasn't thankful for my life.

David nudged my arm, and I had no time to think about it anymore. I had to follow him through a doorway to the left then down a long corridor. It led to a function room, which was already set up with photography equipment. A large white backdrop stood against one wall, and a flash umbrella was tilted, reminding me of the times me and Jenna had shared one just like it. Ours had been big enough for both of us to stand under—one of Dad's friend's old golfing umbrellas, it was—and I'd sung *Singing in the Rain* while she'd skipped and danced beside me. It had been a great walk home from the shop that day, and I decided to use that memory to get me smiling during the next few hours if it ended up being a tiring session.

No one else was in the photography room except for us, but within seconds a young woman came in carrying a makeup bag. And so it went, the usual routine—hair, makeup, hope you're well, what have you been up to lately?—then it was time to put on my first outfit in a small room next door. My first 'outfit' wasn't anything but two strips of white material really, posing as a swimsuit. The strips covered each boob then did up around my neck at the back. I had The Boob Tape on instead of a bra today, so that was okay, and after the makeup lady had dusted my shoulders with bronzing powder, I was ready for the first session.

I went back into the main room. The photographer had arrived, and my first thought was that he reminded me of Austin Powers. He had the same blue jacket, hairstyle, the same teeth, and even the same black thick-lensed glasses.

I smiled when he smiled at me. He put down the small camera he'd been fiddling with and came over.

"Hell-oh," he said, all jolly.

"Hello, lovely to meet you," I said, hoping he was nice.

"No," he said, grinning with his impressive gnashers on display, "lovely to meet *you*, baby, yeah!"

I laughed a bit. I didn't know whether he'd made himself into this character or whether he was genuinely like Austin Powers. Whatever, so long as he made me feel comfortable and took away my anxiety at being so exposed, I'd be happy.

"You're going to be great," he said. "I can feel it in my bones."

He said it like *bownes*, his mouth movements exaggerated.

For some reason I nodded. "You sound like—"

"Austin Powers. I know." He let his top teeth hang over his bottom lip. "Isn't it uncanny?"

Uncanny but sweet somehow.

"Let's get this show on the *rowed*, shall we?" he said, giving me a wink. Then he pranced off back to his camera.

I glanced at David, who turned away, trying not to grin.

"So if you could just stand in front of the backdrop, darling, that would be groovy baby yeah!"

I walked over and folded my lips in on themselves so I didn't laugh. I couldn't be so rude — he was acting this way for real. And if he wasn't and he had some idea in his head that he was Mr Powers, I didn't want to offend him by questioning it.

Just do what he says. Smile. Wave your arms. And tomorrow it's off to America!

"So," the photographer said. "Let's get the lovely members of the public to think you're in Tahiti, yeah?"

He switched on a projector, and I glanced behind me to see the image of a beach. As I turned back to face him, a blast of cold air hit me, giving me such a jolt I almost stumbled backwards. It brought back memories of the hot air incident at Johnny's party and I feared for my eyelashes.

"Look at that hair, baby!" Austin shouted over the din of the fan, teeth dropping out of his gums.

My hair was lifted up then back, streaming behind me as if a gale force wind was attacking me instead of the gentle breeze of Tahiti. My eyes watered, my mouth went dry, and my lips shuddered like they had one time when I'd gone on a rollercoaster with Jenna.

"Uh, I think that's a bit too high," David said, striding to the fan and flicking a switch.

Mercifully, the strength of the blast reduced, and my mouth stopped doing its insane wiggle.

"Sorry about that, shugga," Austin said, blinking fast behind his glasses. "My last shoot was for some weather channel advert and I forgot to turn the dial down."

"Thaz k," I said, which meant that's okay, but I needed a drink because of arid mouth syndrome. "Dink peas."

David handed over a bottle of water. "You're doing great."

His encouragement was appreciated. Had he spotted I was tired, even though I did my best to hide it? Or were my emotions written all over my face?

I'd have to do something about it if that was the case. I only wanted to please him, to do well, to show him that by taking a chance on me he'd chosen the right person that day on the platform. There were so many buskers around every day yet he'd picked me. I'd forever be grateful. Okay, sometimes it was as though he was trying to take over my life, but that was what he did for a living—created new lives and steered people down the right track.

It was just a shame I'd possibly let him down by taking side roads that had a 'no entry' sign on them. Twenny for instance…

You could say I was scared of him—just a bit—but I knew he had my back when it really mattered.

I blinked and said, "Thanks."

"A few more hours," he muttered out of the side of his mouth, "and you can be anonymous again. But not for long there—I've got plans for you in the US."

I'd known it was coming and I was ready for it, but it was going to be great to experience America for the first time when no one knew who I was. I understood now why some stars had two homes. One to live in, one to get away from the world in. If I had a second home, Jenna and Dad could go on holiday there too so it wouldn't be like I'd wasted money on just myself.

"You can do this," he said. "Never doubt yourself."

I smiled, and he patted my arm then walked away, stopping things getting emotional. I was thankful for that. Panda eyes weren't going to work today.

The shoot got underway.

I found that Austin's way of speaking and his persona had me laughing quite a bit, so any smiles weren't forced.

One of the backdrops was a rainy London street, and would you believe it, I had to stand under a golfing umbrella. It seemed that sometimes things happened that could be passed off as coincidence, but secretly I thought they were fate. I'd thought of me and Jenna walking home from the shop in the rain, and now I was doing the same thing. The umbrella had been misted with water, as had the black coat I was wearing, and it wasn't difficult to pretend I was really on that street.

"Make yourself look whimsical, *Lowwlah*," Austin shouted exuberantly, rubbing the tops of his arms to indicate I also had to look like I felt the cold. "Shiver and shake, baby, yeah!"

I wanted to laugh again—this seemed so crazy, so not me—but the more I put myself in situations like this, the more I realised it was me, or a part of me anyway, and just something that came with the job.

How had I ever thought it would only be me singing?

I'd been naïve in that respect, but life was a massive learning curve—a rainbow, each colour signifying something different. Photo shoots, parties, TV appearances, radio shows.

My third outfit was more elaborate—a red dress covered in tiny fake rubies. It was so heavy, that by the time Austin had been instructing me for half an hour in that section of the shoot, my shoulders ached. The backdrop was of a white limousine parked outside a swanky house. Camera flashes hung in the night sky with the stars, and the people behind them taking the pictures were silhouettes.

"Think 1920s, *Lowwlah*. Think cigarettes in holders, men in fedoras...you'd like a man in a fedora, wouldn't you, baby?"

I'd prefer a trendy baseball cap but I got myself into the swing of it anyway.

"Mysterious," Austin said. "Oh, yeah! You look like a million dollars."

That was it. I burst out laughing. Tiredness had won the battle of me trying to get through to the end of the shoot. My legs ached, the dress was too heavy, and the sight of Austin blinking, teeth hanging out to dry, him clearly confused as to what was so funny, sent me into hysterics.

I'd finally reached the point where enough was enough.

"It's a wrap," my manager said.

My tears of laughter turned to tears of frustration. The last few months had got on top of me to the point I blundered out of the room into where the clothes were kept. I plonked myself onto a chair and cried my eyes out from sheer exhaustion.

After a while, the door opened. I glanced up, knowing my face looked puffy, my eyes red, but I was past giving a shit.

"Come on," David said. "We're leaving. It's time to go home."

Diary

Life is Just a Whirlwind

Where is home? If you live somewhere for long enough, that place begins to feel like home. At my place, I've got used to where everything is, and at the end of a long hard day, I want nothing more than to curl up on my sofa with all my things around me.

It feels safe.

I'm home after the 'Austin Powers' shoot and my house doesn't feel as 'home' as it should. No one is here to greet me. No one can come over and sit with me. Roo-Roo's doing some celeb's face before she goes to a party, and anyway, I can't expect him to be at my beck and call all the time. Jenna's doing a late shift at the old people's home, probably getting herself well and truly attached to another resident.

It strikes me that I don't have any real girlfriends. All those from my past—school, the street I used to live in, my busker days—have fallen by the wayside. Part of that's my fault and part of it's theirs. Some went funny on me once I became famous, saying I wasn't the same. Others say they don't feel right speaking to me anymore because I haven't called in ages. I tried to explain that I'm so busy that I don't have time to ring them, but it sounded a load of crap even to me.

I don't blame them for pulling back.

So, I'm sitting here wondering where home is. Whether it's a place inside yourself or a real thing. Or maybe it's a bit of both.

Where is home? What comes into my head when I think of home?

The house I grew up in. ♡

Dad still lives there, won't hear of me buying him another place. Said why fix what isn't broken, why move from a home you love into one you don't?

So I'm going home. I'm going to get in the car and drive to Dad's. Go into his kitchen and make him a cuppa. Get that special smile. Sit on his sofa and tell him how I've been feeling, let him know I love him, then let him know I'm off to The Big Apple.

I haven't even had the time to tell him and Jenna that.

How bad am I?

Life is just a whirlwind.

Oh, God, NYC sounds soooo good right about now.

The Best Cuppa

Dad was in a good mood. I wish he'd retire, though. I don't like to see him working when he doesn't have to. I tried to explain that to him—and the reasons why I wanted to be famous—but he doesn't see what I'm getting at. He says I should live my life the way I want and that he should be allowed do the same. I understand that, and I don't want to come off as disrespecting his choices or even that I want to take them away, but he cared for me and Jenna all those years so I just want to take care of him. Return the favour.

He says he knows that, and God bless me for thinking that way, but it isn't what he wants. Today I agreed to keep my mouth shut on the subject, and he seems happy with that, more relaxed.

His face lit up when he found out I'm going to America on my own for a rest, a bit of adventure time. He hugged me—which I really needed—and kissed my cheek, and as I

left he told me that was the best cuppa he'd had all day.
Huh. It's the funny little things that make you smile.
☺

12

I lugged my suitcase along a landing that had extremely plush carpet. Sweat poured down my sides beneath the sweatshirt I'd pulled on before leaving London. The weather here was brighter, the sun coming out to play, and I could have done with only wearing a T-shirt. It was warm in the main apartment block too, as though windows needed to be thrown open to let in the fresh air.

But it didn't matter. I was here and doing things by myself, going back to real life. The differences in airports had been an eye-opener, though. In London I'd been snapped by people using iPhones, approached for autographs then ushered along by David, who had wanted to see me off, all when I'd thought my no makeup, casual clothes disguise would have saved me. In America, I'd entered the airport alone to no flashing lights, no one shouting "Lola!" and had to wait in the baggage claim area and collect my case myself.

Real life sucked sometimes too, and it made me laugh to myself. Hauling the suitcase through the terminal had been too much hard work, especially as I'd got used to people carrying my bags for me. I consoled myself with the fact that it would take time for me to switch off and learn a different mindset.

I'd managed to hail a taxi without too much trouble, though, and on the journey to the apartment block I'd had a nice enough conversation with the driver. He'd said my accent was *cute* and had asked if I knew the queen. I wondered if Americans thought the UK, or especially London, was so small we could bump into the royal family whenever we nipped out to buy a loaf of bread.

Now I was experiencing real life again by trying to find my new apartment, a place I'd call home for the next month. Downstairs in the poshest lobby ever, I'd signed for my keys, had been given a list of dos and don'ts, and all I wanted was to get in the shower then crash out on what was hopefully a comfortable bed.

"You look really hot," a man said.

He was behind me. As usual, I imagined he was a pervert with piggy little eyes and that he'd accost me any minute. I stopped walking, my heart beating fast, worrying because I was in a strange place, a world away from the London I felt relatively safe in. My mobile phone was wedged in my handbag between a notebook and my laptop, so getting it out quickly wasn't going to be easy.

Who would I call anyway? Nine-one-one?

I turned to face him.

He definitely wasn't a pervert. *Oh. My. God.* He looked like the man of my dreams, all Jude Law in a beige suit—but bigger, and with masses of wavy dark hair. I became conscious of my sweaty self, of how I must look, and desperately wished he'd come along once I'd freshened up and was a bit more glam. A bit more Lola.

"And no offence, I don't mean hot-hot," he went on. "Just heat hot."

Well, isn't he a charmer?

I frowned, remembering that he didn't know who I was. So why would he even consider being a bit nicer to me?

"Er, thanks for that," I said. "I am hot. I'm also tired and pissed off."

"You need any help with that case?" He lifted his eyebrows.

Absurdly, I wanted to kiss those eyebrows, to feel the soft skin there against my lips. I wanted to brush my mouth down to his temple and smell him. I sounded deranged, like some special kind of sexaholic, but he was so...so gorgeous that I couldn't help myself. His suit touched him in all the right places — and I had the insane urge to rip it off. A red tie stood out against his white shirt, and a daydream-like vision popped into my head of his buttons flying off as I ripped that shirt apart to stare at the manliest chest I'd ever set eyes on. I imagined he would have the same fuzz there as my dream fella, and if I thought about going lower, taking a peek at what was beneath his waistband...

What's wrong with me? Jetlagged, that's what I am.

"Um, that'd be nice," I said, shaking the images from my head and realising too late that if he carried my case to the apartment, he'd know where I was staying.

Not that I expected him to want me to meet up with him, or that I thought he might nip round to see me or anything but...

Invisible Jenna piped up.

Oh, admit it. You want him to nip round. You want a man, someone to take you out.

Hmm. That would be okay.

Just okay? A man like him and it's just okay?

With him?

Come on, you know you want to do 'the right thing' with this one.

I did, but not in the way I'd done it before. Oddly, it felt like if I did 'the right thing' with him that I'd be actually *doing* the right thing. I didn't know how I knew that, but I did. Fate, destiny, whatever you wanted to blame my feelings on, I felt *right* standing there with him. I had such a load of emotions swimming through me to do with him. They startled me a little. He'd only said a few words to me, yet there was something about him that made me feel as though I'd met him before.

Okay, so now you're being really *weird. Now you're going into all that romance-book stuff, into girly movie territory. Stop it. It's one thing to want to do it with him because he's all Jude Law and a bottle of rum, but to think you've met him before? Pack it in.*

Before it got stranger and he wondered why I hadn't said anything else, I smiled and let go of my case. But then a thought hit me. *He* hadn't said anything else either, and *I* hadn't thought it was odd. He'd been staring at me—not in a pervy way, thank God—but I wasn't uncomfortable and didn't feel under scrutiny.

I felt normal.

"Um, sorry," I said. "For gawping. I'm tired. Been a long flight. Not shooting on all cylinders. That's what people say isn't it, not shooting on all cylinders? Or have I got that wrong? Is it another saying and I just think it means what I think it means? Or maybe I—"

"Whoa, lady." He held up one hand.

His fingers were long with squarish ends, and I imagined what they'd be like touching me. Just the back of one going down my cheek. Or him curling them around my hand so he could tug me along beside him as we ran through beautiful fields of green where the sun was shining and no clouds were in sight and where—

Wake up!

"Just slow down for a minute," he said.

Oh, hell. Had I said all that out loud?

I took a few deep breaths, embarrassed that I'd probably come across as a woman who didn't know how to behave with a man such as him. But I *was* one of those women and I didn't know how to behave. I wasn't some sophisticated lady who could seduce with her eyes and lure a man into bed with a few subtle, sexy promises. I wasn't in Lola mode now, someone who was more confident than Charlotte but still not confident enough to handle him. I'd been hurtled into being fully Charlotte for a minute back there, and I decided that for all my recent wishing that I could return to just being her, I didn't want to be *just* her, either.

So who did I want to be?

I don't knowwww! But I aim to find out. And who knows, I might find yet another part of me that's been lurking inside that I wasn't aware of.

"Sorry," I said, "I was just —"

"No need to explain yourself," he said, gripping the handle of my case. "If you tell me where this needs to go, I'll take it and be on my way."

I slumped my shoulders at that.

Be on his way? Oh, but I wanted…

He raised his eyebrows at my obvious deflated movement. "What, you don't want me to be on my way?"

Bloody hell, these Americans are so…blunt.

"Oh, umm…" I picked at one of my nails, still looking at him but off to the side a bit, so I wasn't making direct eye contact.

"You want to go for coffee, is that it?" He smiled, some cheeky grin he'd pulled right off Mr Law's face and slapped on his own.

He should get sued for that.

"Hey, I'm not usually this forward," he said, "but you look like you could use a friend."

I didn't want to use anybody.

"Use?" I picked my nail some more.

"Yeah, like you could do with some company."

Oh, sodding hell.

Was that phrase universal? I'd thought 'company' was what Roo-Roo called sex. Did everyone except me know it had a double meaning?

"Ur, just a coffee would be nice, thanks," I said, hoping I'd made it clear enough that I'd really meant just coffee. Even though I hadn't and I could go right along with the other meaning for coffee. "You know, a cappuccino or a latte. With whipped cream and chocolate sprinkles. Not any other kind of coffee. No, nothing like *that* coffee."

He started laughing.

I could lick his teeth.

"What kind of man do you think I am? Try to help a lady out and she thinks you're after something."

"I don't know what kind of man you are. I only just met you." *But I think you're lovely.* "And I'm not after anything." *Except to stop getting myself into these whacky situations.* "So if you want to carry my case, that's nice." *And I can stroke the handle when you've gone. No, that's just wrong.* "And if you want to take me for coffee, that would be nicer." *The other kind of coffee.* "I don't know anyone around here. I've never been here before so knowing a good coffee place would also be nice." *And by a good coffee place, I mean a hotel with a big bouncy bed in it, or even my apartment. Dear stranger, beware. I'm a nympho. Something happened to me on the plane and I've come to America as a bloody raging pervert!*

"So where's your apartment?" he asked.

"Number fifty-one, just down there and round the—"

"Corner. Yep. I know where it is."

I followed him down the corridor, thinking *He finished my sentence!* then telling myself off because it was obvious what I was going to say. It wasn't some cosmic bringing together of souls.

But it feels like it.

Are you sure you just don't wish *it felt like it? Are you making things out to be what they're not?*

"Brit, right?" he said, rounding the corner.

"Um, yes." Should I tell him who I was? No. "Just some boring Brit busker. Nothing special. Nothing to see here, move along, please."

He glanced back over his shoulder, frowning.

I'd done it again. Gabbled. I needed to learn to keep quiet and let my brain engage before my mouth took over and got me into serious trouble one day.

"Why nothing special?" he asked, stopping outside apartment fifty-one.

I handed him my keys, hoping I wouldn't have to answer him.

"What, you expect me to open the door for you as well?" he asked.

Shit. Celebland habits had become more normal to me than I'd thought.

"I..." I smiled. "Please could you go in first in case there's a murderer in there, or a stalker? A squatter or...something like that."

"Wow, you got issues?" He inserted the key into the lock.

"No. Just a bit of an imagination." That was a good enough answer, wasn't it?

"I'll say." He went inside.

I waited in the corridor, watching his backside as he strode down a short hall then disappeared through a doorway.

When he came back, he grabbed my case and took it inside. I followed him into a large living room where everything was white. It was like something out of a magazine.

"These places have all got underfloor heating," he said, tapping his foot on the hardwood. "The balconies on this side overlook some fountains in a courtyard — you're at the back of the building here. When they were built, I...the architect wanted to create the feeling of not being in the city, so these apartments should hopefully be like your own little bit of heaven." He put my case down on a fluffy beige rug.

"You're my own little bit of heaven," I said.

"Say what?" He let out a small, unsteady laugh.

"Pardon?" I frowned.

"What did you just say?" he asked.

"I didn't say anything." *Did I?*

"I thought you did." He shrugged. "Anyway, anyone ever tell you that you look like Sienna Miller?"

"No. Anyone ever tell you that you look like Jude Law?" Where had my ability to flirt come from?

From that throb between your legs, you terribly sudden, saucy little nympho, you.

"I've been told that, yes." He moved over to the balcony doors. "These are a bit tricky to open. You need to turn the key then lift. They should have been fixed already, but I'll just check that —"

"Are you the apartment block manager or something?" I asked.

He hesitated before answering. "Or something."

I was happy with that. I might have to find some issues with this apartment that needed sorting out. "So about this coffee...?" Suddenly, I wasn't tired anymore.

He locked the door again. "Oh, yeah. The coffee. Get that sweater off and I'll show you a good, strong cup."

My knees buckled. "Wow. Um..."

He laughed, but the look he gave me was smouldering. "I meant change out of your sweater into something cooler. The place I'm taking you to gets really hot."

Is it just me, or are there innuendoes flying around everywhere?

"Okay," I said. "I'll just find the bedroom. Give me five minutes."

I scuttled off, thinking that if he followed me, taking what I'd said literally, I'd be doing 'the right thing' sooner than I'd thought.

13

He took me to a diner on the outskirts. I'd been in an 'All-American Diner' in the UK, but it was a poor imitation. We sat in a booth on red leather seats where we could stare out of the window into a car park that gave the impression we were in the middle of nowhere. Like Texas or someplace like that.

This diner was a long metal caravan with rounded top edges and about eighteen wheels. Outside our window stood a red sign on a white post, concreted into the cracked asphalt. A neon yellow light shaped as funky retro writing announced the place was called Teddy's. It flashed, leaving a ghostly impression when I closed my eyes.

We waited for a server, who sailed over in her red-and-white gingham outfit, and she took a notebook and pencil from the pocket on the front of her white apron. Her hair was tucked under a red baseball cap, and she smiled a wide smile.

"What would you like?" he asked me.

I stared at him, realising I didn't even know his name. Why hadn't I asked him?

Because I was too caught up in the prospect of rude coffee, that's why.

I could have called him Jude—I think he'd have got the joke—but for some reason I didn't want a nickname for him. I wanted to call him by his proper name.

"You order," I said, automatically going into Lola mode.

"No, what would you like?" he repeated. "Choose for yourself."

I wasn't sure about that. All these kinds of decisions were usually made for me, so having to think about what I wanted threw me a bit. But I was taking more control now, so yes, I'd order what I wanted — and feel great doing it. "One second."

While he rattled off what he was having, I stared at the menu. Going by what they served in the UK, if I got a burger and chips, that should be enough to fill the hunger gap. I hadn't eaten before departure. And it was weird, but although we were in a diner, at first I'd expected to see the ridiculous meals from the restaurants Lola visited back home, where you paid one hundred quid for a lobster claw, a strip of iceberg lettuce and a midget cherry tomato.

I had to get my mind to shift from *then* to *now*. Nothing in London had to feature in my time here if I didn't want it to.

"I'll have a double bacon cheeseburger with chips," I said.

"No 'please'?" he asked.

I blushed. "Please. Sorry." God, had I become rude as my Lola self? How had I not even spotted that I was getting to be like Deborah? I smiled in extra apology at the waitress.

"No problem," she said. "So you want chips, or did you mean fries? I'm thinking you're from England, right?"

"Yes. Oh, fries. Please."

Off she breezed, and I stared out of the window so I didn't have to look at him — so that he couldn't see my shame. I was struggling to keep my emotions from bubbling over and to quickly sift through some things in my head that had cropped up regarding my rudeness. I was scrambling to figure out when I'd changed personality but couldn't pinpoint the exact time or event. Had Lola Life just crept up on me, settling inside me without me even realising how much it was there? Charlotte would never have been so—

"Are you okay?" he asked.

"Not really," I said, turning to face him. Wow, had I swallowed a wanting-to-be-honest pill? Brits usually said, 'I'm fine, thank you.'

My belly went all funny. He was so good-looking that I couldn't believe I was sitting there with him. I saw gorgeous people all the time, but this bloke? The best I'd ever seen. He beat my dream man hands down.

"So what's up?" He drew a salt shaker shaped like a banana towards him and started fiddling with it.

Why a banana?

"I'm tired." I smiled. "Long flight. I'll be all right once I've had some sleep."

He nodded. "Sure you will. Mind if I ask what you're over here for?"

"Oh, just a holiday." Then, lifting my hand to make air quotes, I said, "To find myself."

"Ah, that can be liberating but at the same time mighty dangerous. I've tried it myself." He glanced down at the salt shaker. Bit his lip.

He'd tried to find himself too? It didn't seem as though he would have needed to. Appearances were definitely deceptive. "Did it work?"

He spun the banana around and around. "Do I seem as if I've got it all figured out?"

He lifted his head and stared right at me.

Oh my God.

"Yeah, you do," I said. "Like you know exactly who you are." *Like you never have a problem in making decisions or fitting in.*

"Then that's where you'd be wrong." He winked. "And hey, this coffee we're having is turning into a meal, and people talk about themselves over meals so—"

"Oh, God! I ordered food, didn't I? I'm so sorry. I didn't think. I didn't realise..." *Why didn't I listen to what he was ordering for himself?*

"It's okay. You want to eat, then you eat. Me? Not that hungry."

I was starving, but could I sit there and scoff my head off while he sat and watched? What if I got melted cheese all down my chin or tomato sauce on my nose? What if the sesame seeds off the bun stuck to my lips and made it look like I had some hideous kind of disease? What if...?

I wondered if I'd ever get rid of these insecurities. Maybe they were just me. Maybe I needed to accept them and get on with things as best I could. And *maybe* if he'd stop playing with that banana I wouldn't keep imagining he was playing with his—

"What's your name?" I asked, blushing harder.

"Blake Hudson."

"That's nice."

He chuckled. "You Brits are funny. Everything is nice."

"And you Americans always say everything is awesome."

"We do?" His eyes widened.

"Yeah, you do on the TV programmes I've watched."

"Programmes?"

"Shows."

"Right." He pushed the banana aside.

Thank goodness…

"So, most people talk over meals, right?" he said. "They talk about their lives. Tell me about yours."

Shit.

I really did want to tell him who I was, honestly I did. Not so he could fawn all over me or anything, but because I wanted him to know me and…what else could I tell him? "My name's Charlotte and I'm from London. I've got a job that screws with my head, so I came out here to get some rest."

"What do you do?" He propped his cheek in his hand and leant forward.

"A bit of everything really. Photography—"

"For real? I love taking pictures too."

His interruption had saved the day. I'd been about to lie, and for some reason that made me uncomfortable—to lie to *him*.

"Great," I said, moving back a bit because the waitress had arrived with a large frothy coffee for Blake and one hell of a giant-sized meal for me. "Thank you," I remembered to say before she walked off again.

I stared at the food.

"What? Did she forget something?" he asked.

I looked up at him then back down to the plate. "This is enough to feed four people."

The burger was the size of a dinner plate at home, the width of a nine-inch pizza.

"Want some help?" He lifted his coffee to his mouth. Took a sip.

"Yes, please." I picked up a knife then handed it to him.

"What's that for?" He frowned a bit.

"To cut my burger."

I'd said and done something really wrong—his eyebrows shot right up again and his mouth hung open.

"Are you serious?" he asked, his voice going up at the end. "I meant help eating it."

To cover my overwhelming embarrassment and the need to hightail it out of there, I took the knife from him and began cutting the burger into quarters, my cheeks flaming. He must have thought I was a total jerk or whatever it was they called ignorant people around here. The way he spoke to me kind of hurt, though. I'd heard Americans were bolder than us, but it was as though he had no tact, no filter.

Isn't that partly why you came here, though?

Invisible Jenna thumped down onto my shoulder, seemingly settling in for the duration.

Yes, but…

He's not being rude, he's being what's called forthright. He's probably used to women doing things for themselves. Then you came along.

I keep forgetting I'm not Lola.

So remember. You wanted real life – you've got real life.

"Tell me something," he said. "Are you some kind of titled person in the UK?"

If he knew that I was a singer, a person who'd been slummin' it her whole life before stardom struck, he never would have said that. But it gave me a shock. Did I seem to him that I felt entitled? That I expected the royal treatment?

"No," I said. "Maybe we just do things differently in London." That was what Roo-Roo would call outright Eau de Bullshit, but I couldn't think of anything else to say.

"Maybe." He nodded then took another long sip of his coffee. It gave him a cream moustache.

Which I wanted to lick.

What's with all the licking?

I don't know, do I! Go away. Leave me alone for a minute.

I was annoyed with myself, not with Invisible Jenna.

"Cultural differences?" I suggested, hoping it sounded plausible and it would take my mind off of that cream.

"Could be." He licked it off.

I want to be that tongue.

He ran a hand through his hair. "But you'll learn here that unless you're the president or you're famous, acting entitled or like you should be waited on won't go down very well."

"Thanks for the warning." So I'd have to learn to be a different me all over again while I took my holiday — more like Charlotte but with confidence. I could do that. I'd had enough practise the past few months. "That looks soft, by the way." *Oh, shit...*

He looked puzzled. "What does?"

"Um...ignore me." I squashed a few fries into my mouth.

"No, I want to know what you meant."

I busied myself taking a huge bite out of the burger, feeling the slap of a lettuce strip attaching itself to my chin. With my mouth full, and holding the burger up to cover the lower half of my face, I stared out of the window and snagged the lettuce off.

"You're eating to avoid answering me," he stated.

God, he was good.

I bit off some more.

"And you think that by doing it again, I'll forget what you said and we'll talk about something else. But I want to know what looks soft."

I shook my head as an answer to try to get him to understand I'd meant his hair. I chewed then swallowed. How could I tell him I hadn't meant to blurt that out? But, he was just so easy to be with, I hadn't given it a second thought before I'd spoken.

Invisible Jenna groaned. *Are you going on about that soul mate rubbish again?*

I ignored her. "Your hair." I thought of a way to make my statement innocent. "And I was thinking maybe you put something on it. Mine's a bit dry, see, so I could do with knowing what you use."

You are such *a moron!*

I crammed my mouth full again. I probably looked like a pig, but at that point I just needed something, anything to stop me from speaking.

"Boy, you're hungry," he said, staring at my mouth. "I love seeing women enjoy their food. All this salad and calorie-counting stuff… Does nothing for me. But to answer your question, I don't put anything on my hair."

I swallowed again. "Oh. Right." Crisis averted.

"You have ketchup on the side of your mouth." He pointed at my face. Shifted his elbow across the table so his finger came closer.

Jenna! Help meeeeeeeee! He'sgoingtotouchme. Oh, God in daydream heaven, he's going to touch me.

He touched me.

I shrieked and a speck of remaining burger flew out of my mouth and landed on his shirt, right beside a button. I swallowed, reached out to flick it off, panicking that he'd think I was the world's worst coffee date, and ended up smearing tomato sauce from my finger down the side of his tie. Thank God it was red too and would hardly be noticed.

"Oh, bloody hell!" I said. "I'm so sorry." I dumped the burger onto the plate. "I'm such a clumsy cow.

Here…" I grabbed some napkins. "Let me sort that out for you."

I lunged over the table, almost knocking his coffee over, and began swiping at his tie. He held up both hands as if to ward me off, and I should have taken it as a warning sign, but me being me, I carried on regardless. I dabbed at the tie. The space between my seat and the table was narrow so I didn't have much room to move. I lost my balance and saw myself lurching towards him in slow motion. A quick flash of the disaster I was about to create went through my mind — burger squashing on my T-shirt, my face firmly planted against his chest, my bum sticking out, my hands landing God knew where.

But he caught me just before I reached him, holding me by the shoulders, my hands splayed over his chest.

I panted — *oh, God, I have burger breath* — his mouth an inch away from mine. He stared into my eyes as I searched his for some kind of inkling that what I'd done was okay and that he wasn't annoyed with me. Creases appeared at the corners, and I saw the tops of his cheeks rise where he must have smiled.

"You are one hell of a crazy woman," he said, his voice low.

I've blown it.

I opened my mouth to let out a stream of apologies.

"Don't say a word," he said. "Just for one goddamned second, don't say a word."

Then he licked the tomato sauce off my chin.

Aj%fhg*fgrurf?hjf.

"Bet that doesn't taste as good as you," he whispered.

"And it's a good job I love crazy." He licked my bottom lip.

My legs went weak. "I…" Was that my heart or some nutter banging a drum?

"We're leaving," he said. "I'm going to take you to your apartment, wait for you to get changed — you have sauce on your T-shirt — you're going to grab a jacket, then I'm going to show you around for a while. Any objection to that?"

I shook my head. I was trying to get my mind around how close we were, that I was touching him and he was touching me.

"Good," he said, pushing me back gently. "I'll go and get the check."

I sat down, dumbly staring at him as he walked to the counter. My legs had gone weaker. And now I couldn't catch my breath. And wasn't that what I'd wanted when daydreaming? Hadn't I said that when a man could make that happen to me, I'd have found my soul mate?

Invisible Jenna flicked my ear. *Well, maybe you've found him. Now you just need to hold on to him and never let him go. Surely you can do that without messing it up, can't you?*

I didn't know, but with a lightness in my heart that I hadn't felt in absolutely ages, I knew I'd be giving it a bloody good try.

The ketchup incident reminded me of another time I'd made a fool of myself with food. Although I couldn't eat in private forever, it seemed I still needed to learn how to behave…

Note to self — eat when you get home!

So it was midnight. I'd gone straight from a gig to the infamous Valentine's ball and I was bloody starving! All that was at this party was champagne. Unless I found something to eat, I knew I was going to end up passing out on the glittery love heart dance floor.

Then I remembered that I had my pizza app on my phone and they didn't stop deliveries until one. Woooo. I wouldn't die of starvation after all.

I glanced around the room at the four hundred or so people and realised it would be unrealistic to ask everybody if they wanted food. Thinking about it, it would probably have sent the pizza company into an early grave, so I went ahead with my single order of a super supreme with extra BBQ sauce and some cheesy garlic bread. I was salivating just putting my card details in. I literally couldn't wait.

Half an hour passed by while I was on the edge of the dance floor staring at the delivery sand timer on my phone, which said it should have arrived by now.

Then, from the corner of my eye I saw a short little Turkish man holding my steaming hot box of revitalisation.

I. Was. Starved! I ran over, grabbed the box, opened it up and dug in. It tasted so good. I'd never had a tastier meal.

As I swallowed the first bite, my body began to feel normal again. I glanced up and to my horror saw all of the guests staring at me like I'd killed someone.

Couldn't I have just waited an hour and saved myself utter humiliation?

Never again. You go hard or go home in this world.

Eating's cheating – apparently.

14

We'd walked hand in hand for what seemed like miles. It didn't feel awkward, just *right*, and we chatted about anything and everything. Blake knew a lot about Manhattan, and he also took me on a tour in a taxi, pointing out landmarks and whatnot. The buildings were freakishly high, and I kept thinking they'd topple down at any minute, that surely they couldn't stay upright. And what if a big gust of wind blew?

I didn't want to think about that.

He took me down many streets, and every so often, the cage-like structure of a bridge could be seen. He said it was called Queensboro.

"You want to go there?" he asked.

"I don't want to get on it," I said, a bit daunted by the size of it. I'd never seen a bridge so big in my life.

"Er, with all the traffic on there, I wouldn't want to get on it if I wasn't in a car either. But we can go under it."

"What? On the water?" I didn't think I fancied a boat ride. My stomach was in knots just by being with him.

He laughed. "No, to dinner."

He whistled for a cab that took us back to my apartment.

On the way he said, "Wear a *nice* dress."

"Oh, I'll have to see if I've brought anything *awesome* with me."

I had. I must have had a sixth sense while packing, as I'd put in the black dress from the music award ceremony. David had said that if his US contact was in NYC while I was there, it might be just as well that I meet up with him for a chat about where my career was going. I'd been surprised he'd suggested that—did he really trust me enough to go to dinner and speak about my US exposure without anyone else there? It was more likely that I'd just be chatting with him in general so he could get a feel for what sort of person I was.

I didn't want to meet anyone to do with my job while in NYC. I wanted to see Blake again and again—and no one else. It was so weird yet so right that we got along as well as we did. It reminded me of how I'd fallen so easily into my friendship with Roo-Roo. Instant bonding, instantly something to talk about all the time.

I couldn't believe I'd only been in The Big Apple for a matter of hours. It felt as though I'd been there for weeks—and that I'd known Blake for weeks.

In the foyer of the apartment block, Blake said, "I'll just go and get changed myself."

"Oh, so you get to live here as part of your job?" I asked.

"Yeah, cool, huh?" He grinned.

"Very! These are nice places. The fact you get one of these kinds of apartments just for being a building manager or whatever... In the UK, I think you'd probably only get two rooms or something." I was guessing, but the apartments were what I'd call mega posh, somewhere Madonna or Mariah Carey would stay.

But you're staying in one. Do you see yourself as different from them?

Aww, Jenna, of course I do. I'm...

Once again, I didn't know what I was.

We went our separate ways, and while I showered, I imagined him doing the same in his apartment. How strange life was. The last time I'd thought about a man in the shower he hadn't really existed—and I hadn't thought I'd stand a chance of meeting a real man anytime soon. Now, in the blink of an eye, I'd *met* a real man and found him so attractive I was contemplating—

No. I wasn't going there. Any erotic moments to do with him would be done with him present.

I dressed quickly, pleased the couple of bites of burger and the few fries I'd eaten hadn't set up home around my waist. The music award dress fitted me nicely, even without control knickers or duct tape. I was letting my boobs loose to their heart's content—and it didn't bother me.

Why was that?

As I brushed my hair then swept it into an up-do, I found the answer. My time with Blake so far had been *that* comfortable, I felt he wasn't viewing me as a sex object but as a woman. Our…closeness in the diner had been a revelation. No one had ever made me feel that way with only a few words.

My skin tingled at the memory, so if we got close again I was going to melt into a puddle. Or quiver and moan, film character style.

I applied makeup—no false eyelashes for me tonight—and went for the understated option. I wasn't an expert like Roo-Roo, but I didn't think I looked too bad. And besides, if Blake found me attractive—and it seemed he had—even with dinner all over my face, I maybe didn't have anything to worry about.

I put on some lipstick, realising with a bit of a jolt that something had happened to me since I'd met him. I'd discovered a new part of myself that I hadn't thought would ever come out—hadn't thought it was ever there.

A smidgen more of confidence.

I didn't have bucketfuls of it, but there was enough that I knew Blake would like me no matter what. That was really odd to *know* something as though it was fact, and I'd think about it more later when I climbed into bed, but *know* I did. I'd like him even if he wore a pair of old scabby jogging bottoms and a holey T-shirt. I just liked him and that was that.

More than like.

I had to agree with that. It was like, admire, fancy, want…so many things that took me by surprise, now I was thinking about it. I thought of what Blake saw when he stared at me. The smattering of freckles over the bridge of my nose that Roo-Roo or other makeup artists covered up so they didn't show. My hair, the lightness of it, the waviness, the sunny yellow tint that Dad always called 'beachy blonde'. My skin, tanned courtesy of the salon down the road from my house. My green eyes—moss coloured, Roo-Roo had said. All those things belonged to the face of a woman who sang her heart out and moaned to herself most of the time about the life she'd always wanted being…not what she wanted.

Yet here? Now? This was more like it. I felt so very different, and all in a short space of time.

Then the old anxieties crept in.

What if it wasn't Blake making me feel like this? What if it was because I was away from all the drama, the pressure, and in holiday mode?

No. I wouldn't have that. He'd been a gentleman throughout the tour. He'd put me at ease, made me feel like I'd tramped the streets with my best friend. Put me in my place if I'd slipped into Lola Land—and I'd *liked* him telling me off. It made me real again—made me realise that no matter how I'd been behaving in London, that being real—true to who I was—was what I was supposed to have done all along.

With Blake had come a sense of freedom, of knowing that I could say and do anything I wanted and only he was there to take any significant notice. The Big Apple with its imposing buildings, its streams of traffic and that scary, huge old bridge, was a balm to my bruised soul.

You can tell I'm a songwriter...

I smiled at my little joke, thinking I could get a fair few songs written while I stayed here. Lately, the words had been drying up. It had been a struggle to get anything decent down. Now my mind was overflowing with melodies and words that streamed through me. It reminded me that while I'd been settling into the role of Lola, my creativity had been rinsed away, down the drain and into the gutters of a seedy London life in the bubble that was Celebland.

I'd popped the bubble. I'd escaped. And, God, I felt so free.

A chime wavered through the apartment, and I realised it was the doorbell. Quickly, I scooted barefoot down the hall and opened the door. Blake stood there, all dressed up in another suit, but this time it was black, his tie grey, his shoes so shiny I could see an elongated reflection of myself as I stared down at them.

Either this man got paid a lot for looking after these apartments, or he'd recently won the lottery. Even I knew the cut of his suit meant it wasn't off the rail.

"Wow," he said, eyeing me up and down. "That dress... Are you sure you're not some titled person?"

"No," I said. "Someone bought it for me." I wasn't lying either—and it was important to me that I didn't lie on purpose.

But is not telling him who you really are lying?

Lying by omission?

Yes, that.

"I could say the same about your suit," I said, taking his hand and leading him inside.

"What, this old thing?" He tugged at the lapel. "Perk of the job."

"Some job," I said, leaving him there as I walked back to the bedroom with a spring in my step and a giddy head and belly.

This was *insane*. I was acting as though I *knew* him. Him standing by the front door was so natural. Me being here... Okay, it was going to sound freaky, unbelievable, but...it was as though I'd always lived in the apartment. Like my life in London had never existed, only in my head. All I could see was NYC, Blake, this place, the streets—and everything else had vanished inside a few hours.

I sat on the bed to digest that.

"What the hell?" I whispered.

Don't think about it. Don't question it. Just go out and have fun. Be you. Find you. Find him. Know him.

I got up, collected my shoes then walked back out into the hallway. We were metres apart and stared at each other, just stared. What was he thinking and feeling? The same as me? And if he was, was he as accepting as I was that this...whatever it was had happened so quickly?

What if he isn't? What if it's only me who feels this way?

If it was, I'd deal with it as I did with everything else. But this time I wasn't going to keep questioning things. I was going to take whatever moments he could spare to be with me. If he wanted to see me again after tonight, then I'd meet him. And if he didn't?

I'd have to cope, wouldn't I?

"You really are lovely," he said.

My chest hurt. Air expanded in my lungs. I didn't feel like Charlotte or Lola, clumsy and worried, insecure and fragile. I felt…oh, I don't know, empowered. As though something had clicked in my head and this was where I was supposed to be, where my whole life had been heading all this time.

It was mad. Fantastical. The logical side of me argued that this would be a fleeting romance and nothing more. But my heart? It knew more than my head.

"You're lovely yourself," I said, wanting to add that he was tasty, fit, lush, gorgeous and all the other words that had clustered into my head since I'd first set eyes on him.

"You'll want a jacket," he said, his voice hoarse.

Did he have a cold coming?

I walked towards him, not to the bedroom to get the jacket. I didn't need one, not if I was with him. Just being with him would keep me warm.

You've swallowed Gone with the Wind, *haven't you?*

Once I reached him, I stared up at him, his over-six-foot height making me seem small and dainty. He opened his arms and I walked into them, pressing my face against his chest. I closed my eyes as he held me tightly, and I waited to feel the same way I had with Twenny and the footballer. Yeah, I was being embraced and was less alone like I'd been with them. But something here was completely different.

I *wanted* to do the right thing for me. I didn't think for one second that if I did it would be wrong. That I'd have to deal with guilt and disgust with myself the next day.

Yet at the same time, although I could have gladly led him to the bedroom—and I was desperate to know what he felt like, how our bodies would fit together—I also wanted to wait.

But what if he doesn't want to see you after tonight?

Oh, he does, Jenna. I just know he does.

You're living in fairyland, sister.

He stroked my hair. "What do you have planned for tomorrow?"

"Nothing." I breathed in his smell—deodorant and aftershave, no idea what kind.

"Want to make nothing into something?" He brushed four fingers down my cheek then slid one under my chin. He lifted my face so I had to look up at him. "Because, Charlotte Whatever-Your-Other-Name-Is, I'm already thinking about how many times I can see you while you're over here. And that doesn't usually happen to me."

In your face, Jenna!

"It doesn't?" *I could stare into his eyes forever.*

"No, it doesn't. I...don't normally get so...close to someone so quickly."

My legs went weak again. I couldn't breathe again.

"So can I pick you up?" he asked.

Oh my God—he's a real Mr Right and he's going to pick me up in his arms and carry me down to the street.

"If you like," I said, waiting for him to do just that.

"I do like." He kissed the top of my head and breathed in. "So I'll pick you up at ten in the morning? Would that be okay?"

Oh, he'd meant pick me up *pick me up.*

I blushed—really hard.

"That's fine." I smiled, probably looking all goofy and stupid.

"But first there's tonight," he said, stepping back so we stood a couple of inches apart. "Dinner at Gianni's. At the bridge."

"Oh, I bet it's lovely there."

He stared at me again. For a long time. "Oh…" He turned away for a second, closing his hands into fists. "You're… I'm… For goodness sake! Let's get out of here before I goddamn *ravish* you."

And then my soul truly knew.

15

Gianni's had an unassuming address for an ultra-impressive venue. I hadn't been anywhere close to something so elegant in a while, and the outside of it told me I'd need to be on my best behaviour. I dreaded to think of the mistakes I'd make once we ventured inside. It seemed as though breathing too loudly would be an error.

The brick façade appeared golden from the lighting, which was sparkly white fairy lights draped over shrubs, bushes and trees. Big white balls — *that's enough of that* — on top of silver posts gave yet more illumination. The arched windows were huge — about five or six times taller than me — individual square panes that glittered, reflecting light from inside and out. The Queensboro Bridge loomed off to one side, its structure so large that it frightened me a little. I'd seen the bridges over the Thames, but this one? It was too extraordinary for words. And thinking of the Thames brought on a smile. My fantasy man had taken me to his boat there, and the parallel wasn't lost on me.

Inside the building, I clutched Blake's hand, altogether freaking out as I took in my surroundings. We stood in a little area with wooden flooring and spotlights set into a white wall. Steps to our right led up to the biggest foyer in the world. The cream tiles on the floor made it look massive, and the waist-height tables covered in white tablecloths, each with a burning candle on them, the brown sofas and squat stools, were filled with people. A turquoise wall at the back was home to a silver bar that had me needing an alcoholic drink so badly I could have grabbed one of the glasses sitting in a row on top and demanded it be filled.

How could Blake afford to take me here?

"We'll go Dutch," I whispered as a man came towards us.

"No, we won't," he said. "Ah, Connor. Great to see you."

The man, who had ginger hair in a gel-swamped comb-over, widened his eyes as he stared from me to Blake. "Lovely to see you have company."

There's that word again. I'll have to ring Roo-Roo at some point to check on that.

"Up to anything much?" Blake asked.

I was a bit miffed he hadn't introduced me — and, to be honest, momentarily confused as to why Ginger hadn't been more surprised at whom Blake's company was. Then I remembered I wasn't in London. I'd slipped so easily back into thinking my surroundings immediately made Lola reappear.

"No," Ginger said. "You need to visit Dad, by the way. The old man's been asking me where you've been hiding lately."

They're brothers? Bloody hell, one must take after the father and the other the mother, because there's no resemblance between them at all.

"So," Ginger said, "are you going to continue to be rude?" He looked my way.

"And are you going to continue to poke into my business?" Blake asked.

They laughed, and I felt a bit excluded. A piece of me mourned the fact that Blake wasn't perfect.

"This is Charlotte." Blake squeezed my hand. "She's my...friend."

"Ah," Ginger said, nodding like one of those silly dogs people used to have on the back shelves of their cars. "Your friend."

"Yes." Blake smiled. "*My* friend."

Whoa. I sensed something going on and although I smiled and giggled a bit, I kind of knew what Blake meant. He was *my* friend, and I didn't fancy sharing him — even with his brother.

"Charlotte, meet Connor, my annoying little brother. He's just about to go make himself disappear so we can get on with our meal in peace."

Connor laughed — a tad too forcefully, I thought.

"Yes, I'm going." He nodded at me. "Watch him. He doesn't do serious relationships, so if you're thinking — "

"She's not thinking anything," Blake said, clamping his jaw shut, muscles pulsing. "And what have I told you before? Don't assume everyone's like..." He paused, giving his brother a funny look. "I want that accounting report you owe me. By Monday."

"Yes, sir," Connor drawled.

There was something not right between these two. It stuck out a mile, but I'd bet if I mentioned it to Blake he'd say everything was fine. Although I felt like I knew him, the realisation that I didn't thumped me in the stomach quite hard.

Like I said, sis, living in fairyland.

As we walked towards a set of white stairs, leaving Ginger behind, Blake said, "Sorry about him. I've known him all my life and he can be...annoying. And I don't want to share you."

What a weird thing to say.

"Well, you would know him all your life, he's your brother."

The staircase curved and at the top I was blasted with the sight of us in the mirrored walls. Warmth sprouted in my belly at how great we looked together.

"Not my real brother," he said. "But that's a long and boring story, one I won't bother you with right now."

But I wanted him to bother me with it. Maybe he'd open up to me about his family some other time. I'd told him all about Jenna and Dad on our cab tour, and he'd seemed to enjoy it. He'd commiserated at the milk and bike story, and laughed at the Jenna's feet in my face story. I looked forward to laughing at some of his childhood tales too. I'd just have to wait until he was ready to tell them, that was all.

We were in a dining room packed with round tables—white tablecloths again—covered in white china and sparkling glassware. There were also tall glass candlesticks on some of them, two standing side by side, one higher than the other. The overhead lights shone, bouncing off the glasses and creating a sky inside, hundreds of stars that twinkled and danced. The arched ceilings made it feel as though we were in the London Underground, and one wall was exposed grey brick. Pillars and a tiled ceiling all brought my busking days back, and a lump barged into my throat, nostalgia taking up residence—the rude bugger hadn't even asked if it could come to stay.

"Are you all right?" Blake asked, gazing at me with concern.

"Yes, absolutely fine," I said, switching my mind to remembering which spoon was for which meal and what glasses were for water or wine. I could never get that right no matter how many times I ate at posh places.

A man in a tuxedo waltzed over, nodding regally to Blake and leading us silently to a table by a window that overlooked the front of the building. I felt oddly calmer seeing the familiar bushes spotted with fairy lights, so stared at them while wondering, as we were standing by a table for six, whether other people would be joining us.

Blake pulled out a chair, beating the waiter to the job, and I sat, still staring through the window. The large leaves of some kind of palm tree stood in a tall glass vase just behind my seat, and the fronds tickled my bare arm. I held in a shriek, at first thinking a spider was crawling over my skin, then relaxed, telling myself there was no reason to be so on edge. I was out to dinner with Blake, nothing to write home about.

But I should be slightly on edge. This fella had a life I knew nothing about. He hadn't offered much by way of information, and I wondered if he felt the same about me. Yeah, I'd chattered non-stop about Dad and Jenna, my childhood, each topic safe, but I'd given nothing else away. Did he feel there were chunks of me missing too?

Blake sat then the waiter handed us menus for wine.

"Do you drink wine?" Blake asked me.

I nodded. "I'll have whatever you're having."

"No, you'll have what you want. So pick something."

He was doing that bossy thing again, but deary me, I loved it. Feeling pleased at being able to do something as simple as choosing what to drink was a sad state of affairs but gave me a lot of pleasure. I chose something that promised to be crisp and fruity — and made sure it wasn't sparkling because I really didn't want to show myself up by burping unexpectedly.

The food menu was next. I picked roast double-sliced fillet of beef with potato comfit, peas and creamed leeks. Blake had the same, the vegetarian option not appealing to him, he said. For dessert we opted for strawberry rhubarb tart, crème fraiche and vanilla bourbon.

As we ate, I said to Blake, "When will you tell me about yourself?"

His face darkened a bit — not like he was angry but more…as though he didn't *like* talking about himself. Or was it that he didn't want to give out any personal information? But it was odd to be able to talk to someone about everything under the sun yet not anything specific about him. Had he been hurt in the past, was that it? Maybe he'd revealed too much, too soon before and it had gone wrong. I didn't dare ask if he'd had any long-term girlfriends, much as I wanted to, but his brother's comment about Blake not doing serious relationships had kind of got to me a little.

I wished for something Blake might not be able or willing to give.

"There's nothing to tell," he said, smiling as he cut into his steak. "Nothing that would interest you, anyway, I'm sure."

Evasiveness flew off him, hitting me so strongly I realised that for all my thinking that being in his company was right, I *really* didn't know much about him at all.

"Oh, I'm interested," I said. "I only want to know what your favourite meal is, your favourite thing to do when you have spare time, stuff like that. Nothing sinister like nosing into your past or whatever. I just enjoy finding out the small things and seeing whether I like them too. Then it gives us something else to talk about, doesn't it?"

He visibly relaxed — so much so that he smiled and let out a long breath.

Blimey, what on earth had happened to him to make him so uptight?

"I can do that," he said. "My favourite meal is what we're eating. I like reading — don't laugh — and watching action movies. I like walking in The Hamptons — "

"Oh my God, you know someone there?" He'd definitely won the lottery.

"You could say that," he said.

"Is it nice? Can we go for a walk there sometime?" I was being pushy and needed to rein myself in. But I was thrilled to have someone I could explore with, a companion who knew the best places to go. "Sorry. I'm just excited. I came here thinking I'd have to look round by myself, but then I met you and — "

"It's fine. I'll take you there." He smiled the same way as Mr Law again, and the edginess seemed to melt off him. "Look, I'm sorry if I seem prickly. I didn't expect to see Connor here. And I'm going to sound like that stalker you thought might be in your apartment, but I didn't want him to know about you. He's...always liked my girlfriends."

Girlfriend? Ah, he's American. Girlfriend means a different thing here.

Deflated much?

"I can't imagine Jenna liking any of my boyfriends that way. We have such different tastes," I babbled, wanting that easiness we'd shared before to come back. "I like Jude Law types, she's more into men like Harry Shields — you've heard of him? The film star? I've seen

Stacey Solomon

him, you know. In London. I was at a party and he—"
Stop running your mouth off.

"And he what?" Blake asked, smiling.

I couldn't tell him he'd pinched my bum, could I?
"Pinched my bum!" Okay, so I could tell him.

"How come you got to be at a party where he was
too?" Blake asked, scooping some peas onto his fork.

"Oh, London's a weird place." I waved my hand,
Roo-Roo style. "Normal people bump into celebrities
all the time."

"Sounds awesome." He ate the peas.

"No, it isn't, believe me." *Crap...*

"How so?" His phone rang. He took it out of his suit
pocket and glanced at the screen. "Apologies—one
second." He clamped his lips together as though he was
really pissed off.

I didn't like seeing him annoyed. Maybe there was
something wrong with one of the apartments and he'd
have to go off and fix it.

"What?" he asked when he answered the call.

Wow. Even blunter than usual.

"Say what?" His face went red. "Absolutely *none* of
your business." He shook his head at me and mouthed
'sorry'. "He had no right. And you have no right,
either."

No right to what? Whoever was on the phone had
made him really angry. He drummed his fingertips on
the table and closed his eyes, as if to get himself under
control. That he was so clearly annoyed didn't scare
me—but maybe it should have. After all, I'd only
known him a few hours and I hadn't checked in with
David, Roo-Roo or Jenna and Dad since I'd landed.
Hell, I had to ring them as soon as I could or they'd be
worrying. I remembered my phone was still on silent
with no vibrate from the flight.

142

"Sophia, I'm busy," he said.

Who's Sophia? A worm of jealousy writhed about in my belly.

"No, we won't be talking about this again." He paused. "Why? Because it's none of your business!" He cut the call, stuffed the phone back in his pocket, then rammed one hand into his hair.

I didn't know what to do or say. So I sat there looking around at other people. I shouldn't feel envious of that woman on the phone, or highly pissed off she'd rang him. But what if it was his wife?

Bugger, maybe I was just someone to pass the time with after all. Someone to have coffee and company with. And I'd gone all stupid, thinking we were soul mates and that fate had made me come to NYC so I could meet him.

What a stupid cow...

Yet there was something between us, I knew it.

"Are you okay?" I asked, thinking it was what anyone would say to someone after a phone call like that.

"I would be if people left me the hell alone," he snapped.

Did that include me? "I should go." I made to get up.

He reached out a hand, holding my wrist to stop me. "No, please. Don't. I..."

I sat back down. How could I not when he was looking at me like that? My mind was full of confusion yet again. I'd convinced myself we were meant to be together. Built the last few hours up as something they obviously weren't—the start of a magical experience. It wasn't his fault I had airy-fairy dreams and desperately wanted someone to call my own. But what about him licking off the ketchup? Friends didn't do that. And he'd said the word ravish. Friends didn't do that either.

Was I just being a fool here? Had I imagined the chemistry?

I fell back on the jetlag theory again. Maybe I needed to go to bed and start afresh tomorrow.

"Listen," he said. "I'm finding this difficult."

Oh no. He *was* going to tell me he was married or something hideous. It all made sense. Ginger's comment was probably to ward me off—that Blake couldn't do serious relationships because he was already in one. And Sophia, she could be the wife, asking where he was and when he'd be home for his dinner, and there was me, sitting opposite with someone else's man and I—

His phone rang again.

"For goodness sake," he muttered. "Sorry—again."

I wanted to run out of there. I wanted to stay.

"You're *what*?" he said, voice so deep and low it sounded scary. "No. No way." He shut off the connection and rose. "I'm so sorry, but I have to go out for a second. I would never do this usually, but I can't have... I have to see someone, all right? Will you wait here for me? Please, just wait?"

I nodded, sorry that our meal was ruined by those calls and my imagination going wild. Sorry that my fantasy was turning a bit too much into real life. Daydream world had been my real world here for a short while, and now reality had come storming along, stomping all over my newfound happiness with its big, stinky feet.

"Two minutes, I promise," he said. "I'll be two minutes."

16

He was more than two minutes. Ten had gone by. I hadn't eaten another bite, and both our meals were going cold. Deflated that the perfectness had been snatched away, I told myself it was all my fault for having such high hopes. Stupid hopes.

There was only so much gazing around I could do before the other diners began to think I was a nosey mare for looking at them. When I caught their eye there wasn't a flicker of recognition from any of them. While I'd wanted to come away to have just that, it was still a bit disconcerting. I really was a nobody here, stuck in a restaurant where the meals probably cost an arm and leg, with no one to contact if I got lost. Why had I thought coming to New York would be a good idea?

Why had I thought it would solve all my problems?

Then a bit of anger stormed into me. He was rude leaving me here like this. He knew I was alone in a big city. And what if I'd got it *so* wrong and he was one of those men who could fool women into thinking he was Mr Charm himself when in reality he was a player?

I was too trusting—*still so bloody naïve*—and I annoyed myself.

I caught the attention of the waiter, who came over and stood beside my chair, peering down his nose at me. I wanted to tell him that no, I didn't belong. No, this wasn't the right place for me to eat dinner at all, but that I'd have him know, back home I did belong—sort of—and that this would be the right place for me to eat dinner—kind of—and he could stop it with his sneer and the pity that shone in his eyes.

"The check," I said. "Please."

"No, ma'am, it's been taken care of."

Oh, so Blake had buggered off and left me but wasn't such an arse that he hadn't paid the bill. Well, that was something.

"Lovely," I said, knowing I'd sounded dumb. "I'll be leaving now, then."

"Oh, no. I was asked to make sure you stayed," he said, flaring his nostrils as though I smelled.

Lola would have stayed because that was what was expected. But what would Charlotte do? I didn't know, but right now I wasn't either of those people. I was someone who wanted to stand up for herself.

"That's all very well," I said, getting to my feet, "but I'm finished with being told what to do."

I brushed past him, feeling every single stare of the diners as I walked near them. Yeah, they could feel sorry for me, some silly, head-in-the-clouds girl who'd been stood up by some gorgeous, wish-I'd-seen-his-banana man. But life, as I'd already realised, didn't always turn out the way you wanted.

I trotted downstairs, scanning the reception area in case he'd got caught up talking to his brother. While that would still have been classed as rude, it wouldn't be as bad as discovering he'd left the building and wasn't coming back. I couldn't see him anywhere, not even propped up at the silver bar, so I took the stairs down to the main doors and rushed outside.

What was I going to do now? I had to find a taxi. The apartment was too far away for me to walk in these heels without getting blisters, and I didn't fancy going barefoot.

I dug into my bag to get my phone. Google was everyone's friend, and it would tell me the number of a taxi firm. I brought up my Google app and began to type into the search box, but a familiar voice stopped me.

"Sophia, I'm warning you…"

Oh my God! The woman from the phone call was *here*? It had to be his wife or girlfriend, didn't it? She'd found out where he was and had come to have it out with him. I was torn between scarpering off and trying to find where they were so I could get closer and see what my rival looked like.

Rival? What the hell was I thinking? I didn't want to be some relationship wrecker.

What I wanted was to go home. And that was a kick in the teeth, wasn't it? All that time I'd longed to get out of London, and I'd come here and found such sweet peace only to discover upset and mental confusion.

Maybe fate had ordered that wherever I went on the planet I'd be followed by dilemmas, mistakes and messes.

Curling up into a little ball would be wonderful right about now.

"I want to see this woman," a female said.

Oh, shit.

Their voices seemed to be coming from my right, but I couldn't see anyone at all. I walked quietly, on my tiptoes so my heels didn't tap the concrete.

"You don't need to see her," Blake said.

I was getting closer — his voice had sounded louder.

"Oh, I think I do!" she said. "The last tramp you were with tried to take everything you've worked for, remember?"

Tramp? Who is she calling a tramp?

I was tempted to stand in front of her and tell them both I didn't want anything anyone else had worked for. That I worked for my own money, thank you very much, and I had more than enough to see me through until the end of my days. So if she was his wife or whatever, she needn't worry, I wasn't going to take a portion of her cash.

And did Blake often go out with tramps?

"She's not a tramp," he said.

"How do you know? You only picked her up a few hours ago!"

Picked her up? What, like I was a…a tart?

"Have you been watching me?" he said.

I imagined a private detective following us all around New York, taking pictures then showing this Sophia woman. That was how she'd known where we were. And Ginger must have confirmed it for her, texting her or something after we'd walked away from him.

But if Blake was married, why would he have taken me out to dinner somewhere so prominent? Why had he held my hand while we'd walked around on the tour?

Bewilderment was my middle name.

"No," she said. "Connor informed me."

So had his brother sent someone to spy on him?

I crept closer to a large sparkling bush, intending to hide behind it. My heel got caught in a paving slab crack and I sailed sideways, crashing into the foliage, sitting on a seat of pine bristles with my legs wide open, dress riding high, and my shoes dangling drunkenly from my toes.

"What the…?" Blake said.

I tried to stuff myself inside so I could hide there until he'd gone away, but the bloody branches waved about as if to say, 'She's here! I've got her!' The wire of the string of lights drew tightly against my nose, drawing it up like a pig's snout and lifting my upper lip so my gums were playing indecent exposure. My hair was tangled in the branches, and I imagined I looked like a demented Medusa. As I began rocking to get enough motion to propel myself out, the branch beneath me snapped, sending my bum farther down and folding my body in half. My knees made best friends with my chin, my arms splayed either side of me around the outside of the bush, and the bottoms of my legs poked out.

I closed my eyes tightly, wishing the ground would just swallow me up.

Heels clicked on the concrete.

"Is *this* her, Blake?"

Oh, God, they were standing in front of me, I just knew it.

He cleared his throat. "It might be…"

"Well, really! You just keep getting yourself into one disaster after another, don't you?" she said.

Another thing he and I had in common, then.

"Do you know what this kind of thing could do to you?" she asked.

"I do and I don't care," he said.

I held my breath.

"Well, you should. Think about this rationally. Think about what the other one did."

"She's not in the same league, Sophia."

"And you know this all in the space of a few *hours*? You're willing to risk losing it all? Based on hours?"

What the hell had they been talking about before I'd come along? Losing what? His job? Would he get into trouble for taking a renter out on a date? Or was she referring to their marriage?

"I take risks. It's what I do," he said.

"Then more fool you."

The tapping of heels again, loud then tapering off. The low chuckle of Blake trying not to outright laugh. The burn of severe embarrassment on my cheeks. And a branch taking that moment to add the finishing touches to my humiliation by scratching the shit out of my cheek.

"Uh, you want some help out of there?" Blake asked.

Oh, so *now* I didn't have to do something for myself?

"No, thank you," I gritted out, determined to fix this on my own.

I opened my eyes and managed to turn — bounce — around and shove my backside out, my shins stabbed by prickly leaves and my arms getting stroked by spiteful little bristly doofers. I reversed until my knees touched the concrete then I had a slapping match with the branches while fighting for the return of my hair. On hands and knees on the ground, I stared at the bush, full of hatred, with the soft wisp of a breeze floating over my feet to further add to my upset that I might well have lost my shoes.

"Charlotte…"

"Go away."

"Please, let me help you up."

"No. I'm fine." *I'm a Brit — we're always fine.* "Go home with your wife."

"My wife?" He chuffed out a laugh. "She's not my wife!"

I relaxed my shoulders. "Your girlfriend then."

"She's not that either. I don't have a girlfriend. I don't have anyone."

They all said that, didn't they?

"So what was she prattling on about?" I panted, wanting my breath back but thinking the greenery in front of me had claimed that part of me too.

"It doesn't matter."

His hands closed over my shoulders. I glanced to the side to see his shiny shoes, the hem of his trousers crinkled where he must have been bending over. He gently pulled me up, and I stood with my head lowered, the back of my neck exposed where my hair had parted either side of my head.

I probably looked like I'd recently had a perm that had gone terribly wrong, my hair tangled and sticking up every which way.

"Look at me," he said.

I turned to face him, lifting my head and gazing at him from beneath lowered lashes.

"Oh, my poor woman," he said, drawing me to him and folding me into his arms.

My poor woman…

No, don't think anything into that.

I kept my hands down by my sides. It wasn't wise for me to hug him back, not if that Sophia woman was lurking about watching. Not if he was lying and she really was his other half.

He stroked my hair, pressing my cheek to his chest. I closed my eyes again, absurdly wanting to cry. How had this day gone from euphoric to disaster so dramatically?

Because it's you. Disaster is your BFF.

"I don't want you to lose your job because of me," I said.

"I won't."

"Then what did she mean? And who is she? And why is she so important it made you leave me for so long in a restaurant?"

He stopped smoothing my hair to cup my face. I stared at him—he was a little gauzy—and he stared back. My heart went crazy. He didn't say a thing, just looked and looked and looked. He swallowed, wincing as though it had hurt, then bent his head and ghosted his lips over mine.

Tears came then, hot and stinging, and I couldn't see him at all save for a murky shadow. I was so tired, not only from the flight but the year of work before I'd arrived here. Plus, I'd built stuff up in my mind to be something it wasn't. Felt emotions that were just the stirrings of lust to be those that belonged to a match made in heaven. I'd been stupid—again—and I was so bloody weary of getting everything so bloody wrong.

I closed my eyes, tears squeezing out between the lids. He kissed them away, every single one. I raised my hands and gripped his jacket lapels—if I didn't I'd fall down. That was how powerful those kisses were.

"She's someone close to me—someone I can't put off with just words on the phone. She's a bit...pushy. Easier to deal with her face to face. And I'm so sorry I left you for that long. Inexcusable and it won't happen again." He sighed. "She's worried I don't know what I'm doing," he whispered against my cheek. "Because I told her some things I've never told anyone before."

"Like what?" My pulse banged *so* hard.

"Like when I met you, everything fell into place."

"What else?" I whispered.

"Like being with you is the best feeling...as though I've known you a very long time."

"What else?" I hadn't heard him right. I hadn't.

"Like I don't want anyone else knowing about you because I want to keep you to myself for a little while."

"Stalker material," I breathed. Smiled. Let my body fill with happiness. "Potential nutcase."

"Clumsy broad," he said back. "Potential heartbreaker."

"I wouldn't do that. Not on purpose." I gripped his jacket tighter.

He kissed my eyelids then pressed his lips to my forehead and kept them there. I imagined us and how we must appear to anyone watching. Me clinging to him, looking like he'd saved me from a wild bear attack. Him staring over my head, into the distance, possibly wondering how the hell his life had turned upside down in a matter of hours, like Sophia had said.

But to me, the image was perfect. I might be ragged, scratched up and without shoes, but a moment had never felt so right before.

"I wouldn't do that on purpose either," he said.

I could only hope we were both telling the truth.

Diary

Minor Adjustments

I am not a liar! Let's just get one thing straight. I might drop a couple of pounds when the magazines are asking or pretend I don't pick my nose when there's no one looking, but those aren't lies (they're just little fibs). Why didn't I just tell him straight away who I am? I'm proud of what I do. I have nothing to hide.

It's just that for the first time in such a long time I've felt normal again. I feel like Charlotte, that fun-loving, easily pleased, simple young lady who could do and say whatever she felt at the time. And I love it.

He makes me feel so normal and treats me like any other person but if I tell him about my other life he might not be the same. He might even just walk away now.

I mean, we've only just met. I don't need to tell him yet, do I? It's not like I'm having his child and planning our wedding. I'll just tell him when it gets a bit more serious. That's if it even does!!!

What if he Googles me if I tell him my surname? Oh my gosh, what an idiot! Why would any normal person do that? I'm losing my mind! He probably doesn't even care who I am, he's only just laid his beautiful dark brown eyes on me. Get a grip!

Anyway, everyone fibs at the beginning of a relationship, don't they? How much you earn, how many people you've slept with—and this isn't even a real lie! I'll tell him if it gets more serious.

I wish I didn't ever have to tell him, though. I haven't felt this happy jelly feeling in my stomach for so long that I want it to last forever. I mean, how would he even find out? Would it matter if he didn't know? Ever?

No, that wouldn't work. If we ended up getting serious, I'd have to come out with the truth. Of course he'd eventually find out. Of course he has to know who I am.

Just not yet!

Best Things in Life

It's true. The best things in life are free.

Walks in the park. Strolling hand in hand along the beach at The Hamptons. Laughter. Kisses on cheeks. Fingers entwining. Hands brushing hands. Secret looks in crowded places. Blushes. Nuggets of warmth in your belly. Curling up on the sofa watching movies. Phone calls in the middle of the night. Intimacy. Shared secrets. Whispers. Learning to trust your instincts.

A week of these things clear the mind and cleanse the soul.

Yet still he hasn't given me a proper kiss.

Getting to Know Him—and Me

I told Roo-Roo that it's not so simple.

He doesn't understand why I can't reveal who I am to Blake. We've gone too far yet not far enough. I can't go back in time and slip it in that I'm a big star in England. I can't say 'Oops, this must have totally slipped my mind, but I'm known as Lola, a famous singer, and I just remembered that I haven't told you, silly old me'.

Roo-Roo's concerned my relationship with Blake hasn't got off to the best of starts. I've told Roo-Roo almost everything about Blake, keeping the intimate, special bits to myself, and from where I'm standing it's off to a perfect start—not counting the restaurant/bush incident. But I know what he means and there's not a lot I can do about it.

Even though I've felt from day one that Blake's my soul mate, I've been sensible and warned myself that it could just be a holiday romance. It's better to prepare yourself for the worst, isn't it? That way, I won't be as disappointed or crushed or devastated (or all those other words I can't think of at the moment) when I have to go back home and leave him behind.

Blake is so funny, he's seen me at my worst (bush incident) and seen me at my best (an evening in a nightclub) and he treats me the same either way.

I've been opening doors for myself, leaving the apartment block without wearing sunglasses, running along the corridor outside my apartment to meet Blake coming the other way because I couldn't wait for him to knock on the door. I've been giddy with happiness. I've been hugged and twirled around until my feet lifted off the floor. I've been told I'm beautiful more times than I could count.

I've been chased along the beach, wrestled into the waves, kissed hard on the cheek when I broke through the surface. I've been pressed against the wall outside my apartment, felt warm breath on my neck and heard the rumble of desire. I've silently begged him to take me to bed, only for him to make a comment that special women get treated with more respect than that. What's that all about?!

I've had my head well and truly turned. My heart is owned by him and I don't want it back. ♡ ← He's held his up in both hands as an offering, and I've taken it knowing from what little he's told me that it's fragile and prone to breaking—but only by me. No one else has inspired him like I have (swoon)—whispers, he whispers these things—and no other girl would ever bring him to his knees like I can if I want to.

Yet still he hasn't even given me a proper kiss! ☹

Random Stuff

Some things he's said:

I love the fact that you like me for who I am, not for what I've got. (What has he got? Not a clue. Don't care.)

I'm so happy with you. (Ditto.)

Commitment scares me, but with you it's not like I'm committed in the way I thought commitment should be. (← No idea what he means, was too afraid to ask.)

I don't understand what I feel for you. (I felt it was a bit too deep to go into.)

I've always played the field, but you're my goal keeper. (I asked him what he meant by that. He said he was the ball and that I'd saved him. Too sweet.)

Some things I've said:

You keep me real. I know real life, I just forgot it for a while. (He frowned at that but didn't push for me to explain. Glad.)

I've realised that if you stand alone as a good person, you can do this thing called life on your own steam. (I didn't add "without going through the whole celebrity circus." TMI.)

Regardless of what lifestyle I have, I think that as long as I'm with you I can be myself. True to myself. Only with you. (I thought he'd run for the hills after I said that, but he stayed beside me on the grass, tickling my cheek with a wild flower. The hill stayed firmly behind us.)

A girl could think her breath stinks when the man she's been hanging out with for over two weeks hasn't kissed her properly yet. (He said the time wasn't right and that when it was he was going to kiss me so well it'd blow my socks off. I don't wear socks but didn't think it appropriate to mention that.)

Something we've said:

I asked him if he wanted a drink.
He told me he wanted a Coke.
So, I handed him a Coke and he read the label, which said 'Felicity'. We looked at mine, which said 'Herman'. He said he'd call me that from now on. We both agreed it was 'awesome' and I told him I liked it when he called me Herman. ☺

Made us laugh so hard. But he told me he doesn't use nicknames with anyone but me because he thinks they're too familiar and he'd be letting people get too close if he has a pet name for them. But he's given me a nickname, so does that mean he wants to get close to me? And it's weird, but I don't want to choose one for him. Everyone else...it's like they need a nickname for me to know who they are, because they don't matter enough for me to remember what they're really called. But I'll never forget who he is—never. So he's Blake and always will be.

It got a bit deep, like we were drowning. He asked me if I was scared and I said yes. I asked him the same, and he said terrified.

A Blast from the Past

Somehow, even though I know who I am in the UK, I've kind of forgotten—until I check in with Roo-Roo, Dad and Jenna. But once I put the phone down, The Big Apple and my life here swallows me up again, obliterating everything London.

So when I opened my email account and saw mail from my manager, it made my stomach roll over.

Still, I opened it. He said he thought I'd like to look at the pictures taken by Austin Powers and choose one from each section.

They're not me, though. Well, they are, of course they are, but they don't look like me. They've been Photoshopped. I seem thinner—that actually feels quite good—my face has extra makeup on it— that's not so good—and the woman staring back at me is so Lola.

17

"What's wrong, Herman?" Blake asked, coming into my apartment, closing the door behind him then taking me into his arms. "Have you had bad news from home?"

Oh yeah, I'd had bad news from home, but not the kind I could tell him about. Even him calling me Herman, which he'd taken to doing often, failed to make me smile.

"I'm just being a bit silly," I said, snuggling against his chest.

"Seeing you cry is painful," he said, tipping my chin up so he could wipe the tears away with his thumbs.

"Honestly, I'm all right." I smiled brightly. "So what brings you here?"

"You do."

I laughed. "No, I mean, how come you're here? Did we arrange something and I forgot?" I wouldn't have forgotten something like that. No way.

"I...needed to see you, that's all."

I knew how that was.

I had two weeks left here, and it suddenly hit me that if they whipped by as fast as the previous fortnight had, it would be no time before I was off home, leaving him behind.

"Where are we going?" I asked.

"I thought we could stay in," he said. "Watch another movie like we did the other night."

"No, I didn't mean that." Much as I hated to, I pulled away and walked into the living room.

I sat on the sofa, feeling like I'd had all the stuffing knocked out of me. That email had brought it home that I couldn't pretend for much longer. I'd be going back to work before I knew it, and everything NYC would become a distant memory, just like London had while I'd stayed here.

How could I possibly let that happen?

He sat beside me, putting his arm around my shoulder and holding me to his side. I leaned my face on his chest and shut my eyes, reaching blindly for his hand. He closed it around mine, stroking my hair with the fingers of his other, and for a few seconds my mind cleared and contentment filled my body.

"What did you mean?" he asked gently.

"Us," I said, as bluntly as he would. "I have to go back in two weeks. What happens then? Where are we going?"

"Shit."

Was this where he told me he'd been lying all this time and that what we'd had — *what we have* — was all a big lie?

"I don't want you to go, Charlotte."

What?

"Stay here with me," he said. "Let me take care of you. I know we've only known each other a short time, but shit, I'm falling in love with you."

I'd already fallen, had hit the ground of love so hard it had shattered every part of me, each piece then glued back together bit by bit every time we'd done or said something new. A bit of my heart had stayed broken, though — the bit that would miss him — and it would remain like that because I didn't think there was any way we could be together if the truth ever came out.

The truth being that I'd told a big fat lie and let him think I was a photographer. I hadn't corrected his assumption. I'd been so caught up in my freedom here, in him, in being the real me that doing the big reveal had been put off time and again because I didn't want this idyll ruined.

Relationships were built on trust. It seemed as though I knew loads about him. He was an apartment block manager. He lived here—not that I'd ever been into his place—and he fixed whatever needed fixing. His brother's name was Connor. He knew people who lived in The Hamptons. He liked expensive suits, expensive restaurants, but wasn't flashy with his money. He earned a pretty penny—or if he didn't, he had a few quid stashed in the bank, maybe from saving up.

What did he know about me—*really* know? I had a sister called Jenna. My dad loved me making him cups of tea. I was a photographer—oh, God, that was such a whopper and it hurt every time I thought about it. I ate hearty food. I was trying to find myself. I was clumsy. Bushes loved me.

"I can't stay here," I said. "But I can come back. Visit you."

"How often?"

"Once every few months?" I winced, hoping he could accept that. I wished it could be more often—and it would be once my career was launched over here—but until then... And what if, when he found out who I was, he didn't want me anymore? What if the drama of Celebland wasn't something he could handle?

If he loves you, he'll handle anything.

Love? Had he got to that stage yet? He'd said he was falling for me, which wasn't the same thing, was it? Could a man properly adore a woman within two weeks? I'd reached that stage, of adoration—the thought of leaving him behind had me in floods of tears, had me empty inside, as if my body had been hollowed out and I was just this shell wandering around the apartment. But was it just infatuation for him this early on?

And how would our relationship stand the test of time with so many miles between us? I'd realised what was really important in life. It wasn't being Lola, fitting in or being liked by people who didn't really care whether they saw me from one day to the next. It was happiness, being wanted and knowing that no matter how you felt, once you were in your soul mate's arms, every bad thing went away.

"I need more than that, Herman," he said then kissed the top of my head. "I have some money put by. I can pay for flights and get you this apartment rent free if money's the issue."

"It's not the money…" *Shh. Watch what you're saying.* "It's time. I get really busy." Before he could think I was finding excuses to put him off me, I rushed on. I had to say what I was feeling in case I never got the chance to again. "I'm sorry to sound like a freak, but I love you."

The silence was deafening.

"A bit," I said. "I mean, I don't want to frighten you but… This thing we have. How can I feel this way so fast? How can I love you when we haven't even…? You haven't even kissed me properly." Well, that sounded grown up, didn't it?

He pushed up off the sofa, taking me with him. Stood me on the floor and held my face in his hands. Stared into my eyes. His flicked from side to side, as though he was looking for something and he had to find it quickly. My heart thundered so hard, and indecision, excitement, need, fear—all of it balled up inside me in case he let my face go then walked out. I held my breath, pulse banging in my ears, and waited for what he was going to do next.

"I haven't kissed you," he said, "because I know that when I do, I'll be completely gone. I'm scared of this...us...the way you make me feel. Everything I've ever done has always been shadowed by my fear of losing it. Getting close to people...I can't do it. If they die or leave me and don't come back... If they lie to me and use me and..."

"You can't live like that," I whispered. "Never taking a chance."

"I know, and with you I've been taking chances every day. And every day you've still been here. And every single day I've waited for you to tell me that when you go home you won't be coming back or you don't want to see me again. I realise I've stopped myself knowing what a proper relationship is before now, what starting to care so much for someone is, and a part of me wishes I'd never met you."

I frowned. "Because?"

"Because now I never want to let you go."

He crushed me to him so hard I found it difficult to breathe. I gripped the back of his shirt tight, the material bunching against my palms. His heart was thudding beneath my ear, and he shook a bit, stroking my back and tangling his fingers in my hair.

"Oh, fuck, I'm so into you," he whispered. "God help me, but I love you too."

The passion in his words, the sincerity—oh my God, I felt every bit of his emotions because they swirled inside me as well. I didn't know how it was possible, but I was devoted to him. It was as though we were connected by invisible threads somehow, that he was a part of me that I hadn't known was missing, and now I'd met him I'd become whole. The idea of being an ocean apart was something I couldn't comprehend. I didn't want to think about it so I just lost myself in his arms, listened to his heart, swallowed the lump in my throat and scrunched my eyes closed.

He was mine — my man, my friend, my forever — and this special moment, where we were the only people who mattered, the only people on the planet, spun a magical web around us, binding us together. No matter what happened in the future, we'd get through it. I had to believe that.

I looked up at him with blurry vision and saw his eyes were glistening. A million things I wanted to say were sent to him in that connection — all I could do was hope he understood, that he could decipher them, believe them, no matter how crazy it sounded that this wonderful thing had snagged us inside fourteen days.

I felt what I felt and there was nothing anyone could do or say to make me feel differently.

He bent his head and the world stopped turning. I held my breath, listening to the raggedy sounds of his, feeling his back expand then deflate as he inhaled then exhaled. The tension, the anticipation of me waiting for him to take the final step, for him to become completely gone, left me lightheaded.

"Fall?" I whispered, voice shaking. "Please fall with me?"

He pressed his lips to mine, kissing me so hard it was as though he couldn't get enough. I parted my lips, and he slipped his tongue inside. Oh, God, he tasted every bit as good as I'd imagined he would. I pushed into him — closer, closer — wanting to climb inside him so we'd be joined forever. I ran my hands up and down his back, learning the shape of it in case the worst happened and I never got to feel it again. I was on fire, throbbing hard and fast, and he gripped me to him, the firmness in his trousers letting me know how much he wanted me.

He broke the kiss to wrench off his suit jacket then smattered my face with more kisses, tiny little pecks laced with the heat of his breath. I reached up to curl my hands over his shoulders, loving how big they were beneath my palms. He picked me up, and I crossed my ankles behind him as he carried me out into the hallway.

He's taking me to bed…

Butterflies fluttered in my windpipe, and I let out an excited moan that at last, he was going to ravish me. I couldn't believe it was happening, even though he walked down the hall, kissing me all the while. It was surreal, better than anything I could conjure up in my daydreams.

Suddenly, a hundred insecurities zipped through my head. What if he didn't like me once my clothes were off? I might be a disappointment to him. Was my bum too big, were my boobs too big, would he like the little mole just below my belly button?

Oh, hell, what if I'm not good enough for him?

It was too late to do anything about it now. Yeah, I could say no, but I knew I wouldn't because it wasn't that I didn't want to do this with him, more that I wished I had the courage to express myself without feeling silly or embarrassed.

I shut those things out of my head as he toed the bedroom door open and took me inside. The door handle slammed into the wall, and he groaned, low and throaty, the vibration of it transferring from his lips to mine. He placed me on the bed then sat beside me, staring down at me as I stared back at him.

I should have maybe felt as though he was inspecting me. I'd usually have been self-conscious. Normally I would have squirmed with awkwardness, wishing he'd turn the light off so he couldn't see much of me at all.

But I didn't now, thank God. I didn't feel any of those things.

Instead, I felt loved, loved, loved.

"I'm completely gone," he whispered, reaching out to stroke my hair, which had splayed out on the bed. "And if we go further, there'll be no turning back. Are you prepared for that?"

"Yes," I whispered. "Yes."

18

Blake pressed one finger to my mouth and traced the shape of my lips. I held my breath, keeping eye contact—I couldn't have looked away if I'd tried. He was magnetic, mesmerising, holding me spellbound in anticipation of what he'd do next.

He trailed his finger from my lips, down my neck then farther to the hollow at my throat. He drew circles there, and I studied him as he watched what he was doing. I wanted to ask what he was thinking, ask him what I felt like—my skin, whether it was warm and soft and if it was exactly as he'd imagined it would be—but I kept silent.

Being here with him like this seemed so dream-like that I wondered if I was really in this bedroom. I could have convinced myself I was having one of my daydreams if his presence wasn't so intense. My heart thudded so hard I'd swear he'd be able to hear it, but if he did, it wouldn't matter. It would just serve to let him know how much he affected me. How happy I was to be with him.

I wanted to talk, to ask so many questions, but he moved his finger even lower, stopping at the first button of my shirt. That action took away my ability to speak. I held my breath, waiting for... What was I waiting for? I wasn't sure exactly, couldn't put my finger on it, but there was a need in me I didn't understand and wouldn't be able to explain. I'd never felt so…alive and aware before.

He gazed up to my eyes, checking if it was okay for him to continue. I nodded, bit my bottom lip, and scrunched the covers inside my hands.

He leaned over to undo the button, taking his time to pop each of them in turn. One side of my shirt slid sideways, exposing my skin, the air cooling it. He smoothed his hand from my waist to just below my bra, the warmth of his palm chasing away the slight chill.

"You're beautiful," he said.

He'd told me that before, many times, but this time it was different. This time it felt like it really meant something. As though I was the most precious thing in his life. I was amazed by that, but if that's what he was feeling, I totally understood it. I felt the same way about him. In the last few seconds as I'd watched him, he suddenly became my all. My everything.

I smiled, listening to the sound of our breathing, the rustle of my shirt as he pushed it wide open. I arched my back involuntarily, wanting him to take my bra off and cover me with his hands.

Instead, he climbed on the bed and stared down at me for confirmation again.

"Yes," I whispered.

He undid my jeans, pulling the zip slowly. The sound of it opening seemed loud, a giant reminder that I really was on the bed with him and we really were going to go further than just holding hands or giving kisses to cheeks and necks. My emotions were all over the place—rushing through me, swirling round and round, showing me in their mad, frenzied journey through my body that I was where I should be. With Blake.

I lifted my backside so he could tug my jeans down, and he pulled them from my legs. I gasped at being so…exposed, even though it was what I wanted. And I felt myself blushing, as I knew I would. He tossed the jeans to the floor then took my hands in his, urging me to sit up. I sucked my belly in, conscious of it, and stuck my chest out a little to give him something else to focus on. To make myself focus on that too.

"I love all of you," he said, as though reading what was going through my mind.

Still, a bit of self-consciousness remained. I wanted to be perfect for him, the kind of woman he'd dreamed about, and with the light on, all my *im*perfections were on stark display. I had to stop thinking about what I thought I looked like and believe what he'd said. If he loved all of me, then I'd have to learn to love all of me too. And he didn't seem to notice the flaws that I was convinced were there. He just slipped his hands beneath the shoulders of my shirt so the collar bowed down my back. I shook my arms free, feeling the material drop away, and all that was left were my bra and knickers. The only two pieces of material that hid the very private parts of me that I wanted him to see, yet I didn't.

He pressed the front fastening of my bra. The cups sprang free and I took the bra off, my movements jerky in my haste. He breathed in quickly, staring at my chest then, with slow deliberation, eased my knickers down my legs, leaving them on the bed at my feet.

He could now see all of me—and the butterflies started up once more.

Before I had time to worry further about what he thought, I reached out to tackle his shirt buttons. My hands shook, and I undid the first one slowly, then the second, speeding up on the rest, eager to see what was beneath. I brushed the fabric aside and gazed at his tanned chest, at the hairs there covering his pecs.

He was everything I'd imagined him to be.

His tie resting against his chest was...oh, God, it was sexy.

I hiked in a breath.

"Are you ok?" he asked, toying with my hair either side of my face.

"Yes," I managed, gathering all my bravery to run my hands up his belly to his neck.

A thrill went through me, beautiful, soft. His skin was hot, almost burning. I cupped his neck, feathering my thumbs over his Adam's apple then raising them to touch his mouth. He kissed them, and the contact set me on fire. He started to say something then stopped, as though he didn't know what he wanted to tell me.

I knew what I wanted to tell him but didn't have the nerve.

I love you. I want you. I need you. Please, just...just have me.

He pushed me back gently so I rested on the bed again. My nerves pinged, and my thoughts scattered, running as if they'd been chased away so that I wouldn't worry about what he was thinking about me. He laid his hands on my belly, his palms warm, the touch seeming to tunnel right through my body. I held my breath again, waiting to see what he'd do next, but he just looked down at my face, a sexy smile tweaking his lips.

"You have no idea how lovely you are, do you?" he asked.

I opened my mouth to answer, but he swooped down with his hands beside my head on the mattress and kissed me, a sensuous sweeping of his tongue over mine, his lips firm. I rested my hands on his back. Did he feel the same sensations I did?

He kissed me with more intensity, time ceasing to exist as we explored one another's mouth. I was lost in him. I smoothed my palms up his body until I could curl my fingers over his shoulders and realised that if I had the chance I would do this all day—just be with him like this, enjoying our closeness. I toyed with the hair at the nape of his neck, loving the feel of it, wishing I had the courage to ask him to do the same to me. To play with my hair, letting it stream through his fingers until it became silky soft. I wrapped my legs around his waist. He lowered his body so our chests were flush— oh, the heat of him was so *hot*—then pulled us over onto our sides. He slid one hand beneath my head to cradle it and with his other he traced a determined path from my throat to my hip. He thumbed the bone there, circular movements that sent desire rocketing through me. An erogenous zone I hadn't been aware I had... God, what was he doing to me? Tingles rushed all over my skin, and I shivered with the delight of it.

I pressed myself into him, wanting to get closer. Small waves of pleasure zipped through me, a warning that I verged on going over the edge.

He flipped me onto my back again then drew me up so I was sitting. I was desperate to see him—all of him—so I moved my hands lower, dancing my fingertips to the button of his trousers. I looked down at what I was doing, my face growing hot. If I stared at his face he'd see I wasn't a confident woman in the bedroom, even though I desperately wished I was.

He threaded his hands into my hair, like he'd read my mind again.

I blew air out in a steady stream and popped open his button before sliding down his zip. I gasped in surprise—he had no underwear on.

"I need you so much," he said.

I swallowed—God, him saying something like that... I hadn't expected it.

I loved it.

"You look so good," he murmured.

Good or not, I shuffled my legs out from between his and knelt in front of him, resting my hands on his chest. I lifted my chin, offering my lips up so he could kiss them. He pressed his mouth to mine, and the kiss was so light, so delicate, it made me want to cry. I coasted my hands up to his shoulders then over his arms, still astounded that I was really doing that. I held his wrists, stopping him from touching me, surprised at my tiny expression of dominance.

I guided one of his hands between my legs. I stared at him, amazed at the confidence growing inside me, then lowered my body onto his hand.

"God," he whispered.

"God," I whispered back against his mouth.

We kissed again, softly, gently, while he fondled me. I held back a whimper as all my nerve endings came alive at once. He cupped my face with his free hand while I curled one of mine around the back of his neck, the other around *him*. I traced my thumb from top to bottom.

He kissed me a little harder, and it was so mind-blowing I wondered how it was that I'd never kissed anyone like that before. My throat tightened with emotion. I couldn't quite keep the sound of a small moan escaping.

This was making love, something I'd yet to experience until now, and the realisation that I'd missed out for so long threatened to make me cry again.

He pulled away to look down. Shook his head as if in wonderment. He brushed both hands from my shoulders to my chest. All the while I ached for something more yet wanted this sexy discovery of our bodies to go on forever.

His breath stuttered as I watched his facial expression. His eyes widened and he licked his bottom lip and, bold for me, I inched closer and licked it for him.

He snagged one hand into my hair then, drawing me close to kiss me hard and fast until I couldn't breathe properly and didn't even want to. I lost myself in touching him, kissing him, and in the sensations he created in me. I gasped, the sound chased away by more kisses.

He wrenched his mouth from mine, clamping his lips onto my shoulder, his breath hot and heavy. He canted his hips, pushing himself towards me, as though he was inside me. I helped him rock into me and arched my back so my chest was crushed to his. I wanted closeness — wanted us as close as we could get — and as he bit a little harder on my shoulder, I gave him much of the same, dragging my teeth over his collarbone then nipping the curve.

The sensuality of the moment was like nothing I'd ever imagined. How had I missed out on this? Why had a man never treated me this way before? How had I never acted like this, wanting to touch and taste and tease and be so into someone I couldn't see straight?

I nudged him away, eager to have him. I moved off the bed and he groaned, as though being apart from me was hurting him. And wouldn't that be lovely if that were the case? If we were so in tune that each time I felt something, he felt it too?

He slid off his trousers before toeing off his shoes and socks then kicking them away. With a smile, he held out his arms for me to rejoin him.

Instead of going into his arms, I pushed him onto the bed on his back, not believing that I was doing this, that I was taking the lead. I closed my eyes, feeling so sexy, so loved and wanted, that all my insecurities melted away. I imagined him watching me, seeing everything that I was in the harshness of the light, and at last, I didn't care that I was so exposed.

"This," he said. "This is what I've been missing."

I smiled. Opened my eyes. Stretched across to my pillow and slid a condom out from under there. I'd wanted this to happen, felt a stab of guilt that I'd been so prepared, but he just grinned.

I handed it to him. He tore open the packet then covered himself.

He held his breath.

I held mine.

I looked at him, knowing what he was waiting for. I licked my lips — such a brazen thing for me to do.

"Please," he whispered, his voice hoarse.

I tossed my hair so it rested on my back. Then I smiled.

And gave him what he wanted.

19

"Oh, God!" he ground out.

I hissed a breath through pursed lips, loving the feel of him. I rested my hands on his chest for leverage, thrilled at how I'd thrown caution to the wind and had done what instinct told me to. It seemed I didn't have to think about what to do—my body already knew what he would like, how I should move.

Moisture beaded on my temples, and from between half-closed eyelids I saw sweat glistening on his chest and belly. Heat spread deep inside me, pleasure building. I leant forward and panted, the excitement of the moment sending me lightheaded.

"That's it," he said. "That. Is. It."

I leant down farther, snatching a kiss then cried out, unintelligible words that had no meaning but meant everything, said everything I wanted to say. I could only hope he understood them.

I wanted him so much. I wanted him to never need another woman, to know I was everything he needed and more. That the closeness, the sharing of ourselves like this, could never be duplicated with anyone else. How could it possibly be the same with another person? My deep feelings for him had to be at the root of my need to please him, for me to want him to love only me.

He shifted one hand to cup my backside.

Oh, God…

I could almost blurt out that this was too much of a good thing, but if I did he might stop and I couldn't bear that. Yes, it was too much but at the same time not enough.

I was his — wholly — and he was mine. I'd never want anyone else.

I kissed him deeply, my hair shrouding our faces, creating an intimate, private enclosure. As the long meeting of our lips came to an end, I opened my eyes and we stared at each other. Time seemed to still. Nothing else mattered except our visual connection — nothing. I breathed heavily, as did he, and I shook my head slightly, awed by whatever was happening here — this…this intimate, wonderful experience.

He flipped us then, me on my back, him planting his hands on the mattress either side of my head. I gasped out a breath, looking up at him, again saying everything and nothing. Unable to wait any longer, I pushed my body up towards him, wanting more. Everything he had to give and then some. He lowered himself a little, which took me closer to completion. I wanted to hold off, to prolong the moment, but it was too late.

Our stuttered breathing, the heat coming off our bodies, the feel of his chest beneath my hands — all of it combined into one big wave and I couldn't contain it any longer.

"I'm…" I whispered, unable to keep my eyes open.

I gripped his shoulders, dug my nails into the top of his back.

Pleasure rippled through me, to the point my mind went blank.

I called out his name, heard it as though someone else had said it from far away, thinking it didn't sound like me but some other woman—a woman utterly in love with this man. I sank my nails deeper still. He growled out a moan, the echo of it mirroring what mine would sound like if I let it run free. I opened my eyes to watch him, scoring my nails down his back. The ripples inside me intensified then began to abate, leaving me wrung out, sated, and exhausted all at once.

"Oh my God," I said, out of breath and stunned by the ferocity of our union.

He tipped his head back, the cords of his neck standing out. His body shuddered and he whispered my name then snuffed it out by kissing me. I held on to him, stroking the back of his head, his hair peeking out from between my fingers. A swell of emotion swamped me, bringing a lump to my throat and heat to my chest, as though it had filled with all the love I felt for him and it promised to consume me if I didn't say something.

"I love you," I said, breathless and tearful.

A moment of silence, which felt like a lifetime, then, "And I love you too."

I clung even tighter to him, pushing him onto his side so I could lie flush to his body and hold him tight. I never wanted to let him go. Never wanted this moment to end. I kissed him, a hungry meeting of lips that I hoped conveyed how much I felt for him. That life would never be the same for me now.

I tucked my head beneath his chin. He held me, one hand on my back, the other in my hair, and fiddled with the strands while I got my breathing under control. And I was glad. If he got up now, the spell would be broken and I wanted it to stay wrapped around us forever.

It was a few minutes before I felt I could speak, and all I managed again was, "Oh my God."

He chuckled, the kind that said he was having trouble comprehending what had happened too. I understood how he felt — what *had* just happened?

"Never have I…" he said.

And he didn't have to finish that sentence or elaborate. I knew.

I closed my eyes and listened as his breathing steadied. I drew lines on his back with my fingertips — up and down, up and down — until his skin cooled and my heart stopped thudding so hard. My body continued to pulse, as though remnants of my intense experience were still there, lingering on to remind me that if he touched me again I'd be sent back to that beautiful place he'd just taken me.

"How did I get so lucky?" I whispered, more to myself than to him.

"How did I?"

I smiled, my cheek bunching against his chest. He pressed his chin closer to the top of my head, and I felt completely cocooned in him, completely safe and loved. That dream I'd had, of finding my love — never had I thought it would be like this. My imagination hadn't stretched this far, and the reality was much better than the daydream.

My Mr Perfect…

I didn't feel silly for thinking that, either. He *was* my special man, and the love I'd felt for him before was nothing compared to now. Our being together like we just had made my feelings for him even stronger, and I knew that if he didn't want to see me again once I'd gone home, a part of me would always remain here in The Big Apple with him.

The only thing that soured it all was my inability to tell him who I really was.

I erased it from my mind so this moment wouldn't be tainted.

"You know," he said, "one of my favourite things to do now is to be with you like this. To stroke your hair, to hear you breathing, to feel you against me. I don't think I've ever felt so content in my life."

I smiled, hugging him closer then continuing my fingertip exploration of his back.

"There was a time," he said, "when I thought I'd never find someone like you."

"I always knew I would. Something inside told me I'd find my soul mate. I never knew when, but I definitely knew he was out there somewhere. *You* were out there somewhere."

"Then you had more faith in fate than me. I..." He paused. Took a deep breath. "There have been others, and I thought I loved them. Thought they loved me. But they didn't. How about you?"

"I've made mistakes." That was all I could say really, wasn't it? I thought about how to explain my time with Twenny, with the other two brief encounters I'd had before then when I'd been younger. "I've never had a really long-term relationship. A couple of months at the most with one guy. I thought he loved me and I loved him, but I see now it was just puppy love or whatever." I sighed. "This...this whatever it is we have... It's all new to me. I don't understand it but I love it. It's frightening yet not scary at the same time because it feels so right. I can't explain it. I don't think it needs an explanation or for me to analyse it to death. I just think I'll accept it for what it is and enjoy it."

I felt him nod.

"I feel the same. We should just go with it. And it's mad, but I can't see myself with anyone else. Not now."

I knew what he meant.

"So we're stuck with each other," I said.

"We are. You got a problem with that, Herman?"

"Nope. You?"

"Nope."

"Then be quiet. I want to fall asleep like this."

"So do I, but I have to use the bathroom."

He pulled away, and I felt so cold without his arms around me. He left the bed, and it felt stupid but I wanted to follow him, to be close again. Being in the bed by myself was wrong—I was lonely and hollow, my skin needing his against it.

I climbed under the quilt and waited for him to come back. It seemed like ages before he did, and once he joined me again, drawing me to him and holding me tight, the completeness returned.

Wherever he was, was home.

I closed my eyes, content not to speak and to just be with him.

There was nothing else to say anyway.

I think we'd just about covered it all.

Diary

Note to self: DO NOT LIE (even by omission)

Blake walked past the coffee table and nudged it and my laptop sprang to life. I noticed his frown at what was on the screen and I had to think for a sec what I'd been looking at to cause that reaction. My throat went dry when the pictures crashed into my mind.

He'd seen me in the two-strip bathing suit on my photo shoot and wanted to know if there were more pictures. He looked gob-smacked and asked if he could see them. What could I do? I showed them to him and was told it didn't look like me. Of course, then he wanted to know if the images were taken by me—of me. I couldn't answer. If I did, I'd have outright lied.

I think he was so intent on looking at the pictures that he didn't notice my silence and he complimented me on my photography skills. I laughed, almost hysterically. What else could I do? I told him it wasn't me, not really. That it was mostly makeup, lighting and so on to create a fake impression.

He told me that he liked *this* me better—the me standing in front of him. I agreed. Anyway, I closed the laptop.

Fear is now scraping sharp nails down my back and wringing my stomach out in its fists.

He's going to find out about me sooner than I'd like, isn't he? He's going to know I'm a liar. The trust we have is going to crumble—maybe to dust, who knows. Or maybe it'll snap in two and be easier to repair. Hell, he might even love the fact that I'm a star.

I'll find out soon enough.

But not yet. I don't want him to find out yet.

20

We went out to eat at a restaurant that was Lola's kind of place and Charlotte's worst nightmare. It was as posh as Gianni's but tucked away down a side street. I saw a man—a bloke I'd seen hanging out in London with Twenny Pee once—and my stomach dived south. What if he spotted me? My body grew cold, I got the shakes, and Blake eyed me as though I was a piece of glass that might shatter.

"Are you ill?" he asked as we sat in our seats, thankfully in a far corner in the shadows.

"No, just a bit cold. I'll soon warm up."

And I did warm up once the man had left—seemed he'd only come in for a drink—and I guessed he was in NYC for something or other to do with his music. From what I could remember of the haze-filled night I'd met him—I'd been a little tipsy on alcohol and had had a brief conversation with him about pugs versus staffies—he was an up-and-coming producer. He'd said he had both breeds of dog and had tried to convince me to get one from his mate's breeding farm. I'd declined.

What if Twenny was here in New York too? He was all I needed to see. Things would go totally tits up in a heartbeat if he saw me while I was with Blake and came over to chat. But would he want to chat, though? I'd successfully avoided him since our…encounter, but the fact he held grudges and might have a big beefy one reserved just for me gave me the shivers. I was sure Roo-Roo would have let me know if Twenny was likely to be here, though. He knew ninety per cent of the gossip before anyone else.

But what if the other ten per cent contains things I need to know?

Going out in NYC again after tonight was suddenly unappealing.

I was nervous now, trying not to jump every time someone new came through the front door. If I didn't stop looking dodgy, Blake was going to pick up on my unease and start asking questions.

Which would mean I'd have to lie some more, and since we'd made love, the thought of lying had me feeling ill. Really ill. I had so much to lose, but if I had to walk away from him to save him getting hurt, I would. That sounded nuts but it was true. I loved him enough to let him go.

It'll kill me.

I blinked so tears wouldn't come and studied the crowd for anyone else I might know. I didn't recognise a soul, so we ordered our food. Once it had arrived — steaks with pan-fried chips...er fries — I relaxed, chatting with Blake between bites, talking about what movie we'd watch later. I suggested *Love Actually* and he rolled his eyes, giving in after I reminded him that he'd chosen the last one, some thriller or other that had frightened me half to death. I'd clung to his arm because of it — that was my excuse, anyway — and had covered my face with a cushion.

If I wasn't famous I could stay here.

If I wasn't famous I wouldn't have been able to afford to come here and meet him.

"Do you think we'd have met no matter what?" I asked then took a bite of steak.

"What, if you hadn't come over here?" He stopped stabbing a fry with his fork to tilt his head and look at me.

"Yeah. If I didn't do what I do for a living, I wouldn't have ever stepped foot in America. I wouldn't have had enough for the fare or to rent the apartment." I was skating close to him asking questions but I wanted to hear his thoughts on the subject.

"If things are meant to be, I think they happen somehow, yes. I've been thinking of going to England for a while now, so maybe…" He shut his mouth, his lips forming a thin, tight line.

I swallowed my food. "To do what?"

"Visit." He shrugged. "See if I like the place. Is it nice?"

"You'd probably think it was awesome."

We laughed, but my laughter hid a bout of unease as I imagined him coming to London once I'd gone back and seeing the current pictures of me splashed on taxis and the sides of buses.

"Then maybe I should go there," he said.

My muscles tensed, and I tried to think of a way to divert the conversation elsewhere.

My subconscious was telling me to come clean. Here. Now.

The restaurant door swung open, and I glanced over to see who had come in. I really needed to hurry this meal up somehow so we could leave. This nervousness was a nightmare. A crowd of young men entered, and I relaxed, although my stomach was still in knots. It would be better to suggest meals in my apartment from now on, or to at least go to the diner or more out of the way places.

I looked down at my plate and busied myself cutting a slice off my steak.

"Drinks all round, baby, yeah!"

I sat stock still, the stomach knots unravelling, turning into giant snakes that writhed. Goosebumps broke out on my arms and a shiver zipped up my back, spreading all over my scalp and freezing my skin. I swallowed, snapping my head up sharply, cursing myself for the quick action because Blake was watching me.

"What's up?" he asked.

While staring directly at Austin Powers, I swallowed again, nauseated. "Bloody hell, I know him."

There wasn't any way I could say anything else. Austin Powers bounced towards us, his teeth leading the way. His skin-tight jeans and pointy-toed black shoes, his white shirt with ruffles, his God-awful hair and those black-framed glasses—all of them gave me a series of shocks that left me shaking from head to foot. I made to stand—I had to run, to get out—but Austin was at our table, smiling down at me with his tombstone gnashers.

"Well, baby, I come away for a bit of R and R and bump into you," he said, grinning, his eyes bugging.

I smiled. "Small world."

"I'll say. *Sma*shing to see you. Did you see the pictures? Like them? Did you? Me, I loved them." He winked. "Especially the swimsuit ones, know what I mean, darling?"

Oh, God. Oh, God. Please make him go away.

"They came out really well," I said, my voice not sounding like mine. My fork rattled against my plate where my hand shook.

"Listen," Austin said, waving his hands beside his head and giggling, "I'd love to stop and *chaaat*, but those guys are waiting for me so…great to see you're taking a break. Thought you'd have chosen Tahiti, though! Catch you on the spot next time you look hot!" He waggled his fingers then turned and waltzed away.

Shit. Shit!

"Who the *hell* was that?" Blake asked, turning to stare at Austin over his shoulder.

"A photographer. Absolutely crazy person. Ignore him."

Ignore the fact he came over and almost blew everything.

Blake faced me again. His cheeks were red and he frowned—too hard. "Is he one of the men you told me about? An old fling?"

I laughed—a bit too loudly—and let my fork go. The rattling was getting on my nerves. "No! Oh my God, no. He's a colleague. As you might have guessed, he thinks he's Austin Powers."

"Austin who?" His face softened a bit, although his eyes were hooded and the irises seemed darker.

"We'll have to watch the movie so you can see what I mean. It's a film character. Funny. Weird. The actor plays loads of different parts." *Talk about something else.*

Blake shook his head. "What a strange guy." He looked over at Austin again then back to me. "I got a little…jealous for a second there."

"You did?"

"Hell yes."

"Do you want to leave?" *Say yes.*

"Only if you want to."

"I do."

Our meals were almost finished so I didn't feel badly about getting up right there and then and waiting for him to stand too. While Blake paid the check at the desk, I nervously slipped my jacket on, keeping an eye out for Austin, in case he decided he did have time to talk to me again. He was sitting with the young men in a far corner, toasting one of them, holding up a large glass, the red wine inside sloshing about from his over-the-top arm movements. I shivered, thinking I could wait outside, to be away from everyone in here, but before I could take a step, Blake was walking towards me.

He draped his arm around my shoulder and swooped in for a kiss. I was so surprised I squealed, hating myself for it in case it brought us to Austin's attention. I stared at Blake with his lips pressed to mine, and behind him a bright light flashed. I sagged, automatically thinking *camera, oh my God, a bloody camera* and broke the kiss to lower my head. My need to get out was intense, so I grabbed his hand and tried for the casual look of walking calmly.

A man stood in front of us, a camera held up to his eye, clicking furiously. The string of flashes hurt my eyes, and I lifted a hand to shield them. Blake snarled, letting my hand go, and he leapt forward, arm raised. He shoved his open hand into the man's face, pushing the camera aside and wiping the snapper himself out of our path.

"Get the hell away from us," Blake said, the tone of his voice one I hadn't heard before. "Give me some goddamn space for once, will you?"

He'd sounded vicious, at the end of his tether and ready for a fight. My heart pumped furiously with fear, my mind screaming for me to get the hell out and back to the apartment without anyone following us. Blake grasped my elbow and all but dragged me outside, his breathing heavy, his face red, jaw rigid, eyes wide.

"Come on," he said, leading me down the street with his arm about my waist.

"Oh, bloody hell," I said, freaked out by the ramifications that were going to come my way. I'd have to tell him. He'd hate me for lying. I was going to lose him and I'd have no one to blame but myself.

The pain bit deep and hard.

I held back a sob, scurrying to keep up with him. He whistled and a taxi drew up alongside the kerb. He opened one of the rear doors and made sure I was in first then walked around the back to get in the other side. I stared through the window. The snapper had followed us out and was taking more pictures. I shielded my face, a dreadful swirl of hate for him in my belly that he'd expose me and I'd be caught out in my web of omissions.

"Bastard," Blake muttered. "I'm sorry about that."

He was sorry? For saying bastard?

"Some people around here don't understand the meaning of privacy," he said, taking hold of my hand and squeezing.

He told the driver where we needed to go. We sat in silence for a while, me swallowing loads of times to try to stop myself throwing up. Fear was enjoying itself, rampaging through my body, showing me scenarios in my head that I didn't want to see.

"I've got some nice wine in my apartment," he said. "We can drink it and forget what happened back there." He sighed. "Let's just get home and forget it all. And we won't be going out to eat again while you're here. I'll cook for you or order take-out. You don't deserve that kind of crap."

Did he already know and just wasn't telling me he knew?

I couldn't ask, because if he didn't know, he'd wonder why I'd brought it up.

I started counting to ten in my head, telling myself that once I reached ten I'd spit it all out and hope that things turned out okay. I got to ten then started from one again, repeating that until we reached the apartments.

Blake checked through the rear window then paid the driver. "Stay there a second."

He left the cab then came round to my door, glancing up and down the street. Then he opened it and helped me out before whisking me inside to the foyer.

Relief poured into me, but not enough to completely take away the fright I'd had or the apprehension that this wasn't over by a long shot. There might not have been anyone following that Blake could see, but the press were sometimes hateful and managed to tail someone without being spotted.

If they found out I was staying here…

I gulped down another burst of fear.

"We're home," he said, guiding me to the lift. "I'll make sure you get to your apartment okay then I'll go and get the wine."

We stepped inside. I stopped myself from sagging against the glass wall.

Home. Yes. But maybe not for as long as I'd thought.

21

It was weird how the apartment *did* feel like home. Maybe home really was wherever 'happy' was. Although I was still reeling from what had happened, I felt so much better, happier, by being in the apartment. Safe.

Would Blake's place feel like home if I ever got to go there? It was a bit odd that I'd never been to his apartment, but maybe if I asked him if I could see it, we could have a change of scenery there from time to time. Plus I was curious about his space. How he lived. We'd fallen into a pattern of always ending up in mine, but I was dying to see his. How he'd chosen to put his stamp on it would give me more information about him. I reckoned he'd have all black furniture with blue or cream pillows on the sofa. No curtains, just venetian blinds—black again. I suspected all the apartments were the same layout, so picturing him inside his didn't stretch my imagination too much.

I hung my bag on the living room door handle, so relieved to be back. Blake was still in his apartment getting the wine—something I could do with after the scare at the restaurant. The alcohol would uncoil my nerves, but I had to be careful how much I drank in case it uncoiled my tongue too.

As I stared out of the window down at the fountains, which were lit up by pink and purple spotlights, I realised that by Blake not knowing who I was, there was so much I couldn't share with him. Telling him how I'd felt in the restaurant—how I felt now—would have taken a lot of pressure off me. But I was only feeling that pressure *because* he didn't know who I was. That picture snapper would have sent his images to a newspaper by now—or several of them—and by the morning my very own fantasy man might disappear, never to be seen by me again.

I'd like to say I knew him better than that. I was assuming he wouldn't want to know me due to the fame angle. It went deeper. He would be hurt by the lack of trust and the abundance of lies—at least it seemed as though there was an abundance of them anyway. But it had been so important to me that he got to know me, not my persona, and that him loving me had nothing to do with stardom and everything that came with it. In my line of business, it was difficult to know who to trust. Some people were out for all they could get, and if it meant using a star to get it, they'd do it.

I didn't understand that at all. Where was their common decency, their morals? I was a person the same as everyone else—so why couldn't some people see that? How did they not feel guilty for using someone in that way?

I'd never know—I clearly wasn't made from the same mould as them.

The doorbell chimed, and as I went to answer it, I thought of how Blake had reacted to the snapper. His job must mean a lot to him, because your average person wouldn't blow up like that. I knew he wanted to keep me to himself, to keep our relationship as private as possible, but bloody hell! Who but a famous person planted their hand on a photographer's face and shoved him out of the way? Who shouted, 'Give me some goddamn space for once, will you?'

I decided to ask him about it at the first opportunity I got.

He came in, holding up the bottle of white. His smile looked fake — I'd seen enough of my own in the mirror to recognise he was hiding something — and dread plonked itself in my belly and made itself comfortable.

"Everything okay?" I asked, closing the front door.

"Hopefully it will be." He grimaced then exchanged it for another weird smile.

Something was off. Or maybe it wasn't and the restaurant thing was clouding my judgement.

Maybe he really does know and he's waiting to see how long it'll be before I confess.

I led him into the living room, holding back a sigh because really, now was the time to tell him. Before the images hit the news. But what if he didn't give me time to explain properly? I wasn't ready to watch him storm out of the door. I was selfish and wanted to keep what we had for a bit longer.

He walked through to the kitchen, then came back with two glasses. I sat while he opened the bottle then poured, my mind going crazy with scenarios, all of them with a glass-half-empty outlook.

"Tonight was a bit strange, wasn't it?" I asked. Strange wasn't the word.

"It was annoying." He handed me a glass. "I don't like having my photo taken."

"Me neither." I took a deep breath then let it out. "What did you mean when you said for them to give you space for once?"

He shook his head. Downed his wine then poured another. Whoa, it seemed he needed the alcoholic courage more than I did.

"Listen, I've got something to tell you," he said, sliding his fingertips back and forth over his forehead.

My tummy hurt. Any more scares tonight and I'd be sick. *Had* he found out about me? I scrabbled to find excuses, reasonable ones that would explain my silence regarding Lola. The only plausible one I could come up with, the one that might make him understand, was a true one. I wanted to be myself. I wanted someone to love me for me. Surely he'd get that.

His phone rang, increasing the tension that seemed to swirl in the room around us. It prickled, that tension, stabbing into my skin and bringing up goosebumps. I rubbed my arms as I watched him take his phone out and stare at the screen. He closed his eyes for a moment or two then opened them again.

Isn't he going to answer that?

"What?" he barked into it. "Yes, I'm well aware of that." He stood, going over to the window, his back to me.

I sat helplessly, knowing he was angry—also hurt because he sounded it—not knowing what to do to help him. I also had my own emotions to contend with. If that caller was going to spill the beans, I needed to brace myself for heartbreak.

Why did we have to go into that restaurant tonight? Why didn't I push it and tell him I'd prefer to go somewhere quieter?

My lack of knowledge about the area had been a downfall. If I'd lived here longer I would have known it was a celebrity-press hangout. I would have avoided it.

I wrung my hands and bit my bottom lip.

"I can't talk right now," he said, glancing at me over his shoulder.

Oh. That was suspicious. Unease took hold of my bones, making my legs shake.

"Because I can't, that's why." He paced then stopped at the door, putting his hand against the doorframe and staring down at the floor. "Yes. I know. And that's why I never told her. Don't you *get* that?"

Told who what?

"Your contact said *what*?" He took hold of his hair in his fist.

Oh my God. No. He knows.

My legs went weak for all the wrong reasons.

"Well, that's just fucking great. Hang on a second." He turned to face me, smiled tightly, and pressed his phone to his chest. "I'm so sorry, Charlotte, I need to finish this call in private. I'll just… I won't be long."

As he walked past, putting the phone back to his ear, I heard, "Who the hell is Charlotte?" being said by the person on the other end.

A woman.

Sophia again?

My heart sank. This woman was beginning to seriously get on my nerves.

He headed for the front door then disappeared out into the corridor.

I had to know what that call was about, especially since *she* was the caller.

I crept to the door. A two-inch gap where he'd left it ajar afforded me enough earwigging and viewing space. His shadow played on the wall opposite, moving quickly—him pacing again, I guessed.

"If this ruins everything," he said, "I'm laying the blame firmly at your door."

I swallowed down a pinch of fear.

"There is no way anyone would have known I was there unless I'd been followed. Hasn't Connor got rid of the tail yet? I told him to do that months ago once everything had died down."

I frowned hard.

What the bloody hell's going on? Months ago? I wasn't here months ago.

"She's a crazy bitch and I don't want to set her off, so you'd better get back to your contact and warn them not to go ahead. Tell him to hold off for a couple of weeks until she's gone home."

Crazy bitch? Had I given him that impression about myself? I rather thought I'd been calm and happy.

Shows how much I know about human perception.

And if he thought I was a crazy bitch, why was he with me? Did he dig angry birds or what? Or maybe it wasn't even me he was talking about. And what had to be held off until after I'd left?

"No," he said. "Goddamn it. Get things sorted. I won't put up with this kind of crap, not now. Not when I'm this close." His shadow stopped moving. It bent over, like he was inspecting his shoes. "I can't... I can't do this for much longer."

I felt sick.

"Wait. I have another call." His shadow stood upright. "If you're calling about earlier, don't say a word... What? Oh, this just gets better and better. You're *what*? I don't *need* you to be here. A call would have been enough. And I can't believe you didn't take the tail off when I asked you to. Uh-huh. Right. Yeah, you're right. Okay, I'm sorry. Right."

What the...? My frown was making my eyes hurt.

"I'll be there in a second."

I shot back into the living room and flung myself on the sofa. Blake came in, looking apologetic and something else. Worried? Frightened?

"I'm so sorry about this, but there's something very important I have to do. I know I said I wouldn't leave you again when I'm spending time with you, but someone's at my apartment and I need to go see them. I'll be back in about half an hour. I can't put it off — again, I'm sorry."

He walked over to me and hunkered down, cupping the back of my head and pressing a kiss to my temple. I closed my eyes, trying to keep the tears back, wondering if this was the last time he'd ever kiss me, touch me. I grabbed hold of him, pulling him to me, pushing his cheek to my chest so I could stroke his hair and feel him, be close, to give me something to remember.

"I love you," I said.

He lifted his head. "Don't hate me."

"I couldn't. I won't."

He stood, looking down at me, and I swore he was about to say goodbye.

"Half an hour." He walked out.

I could have crumpled, cried, given in to fear and heartbreak, but something propelled me to my feet. I followed him out, catching sight of his jacket hem as he rounded the corner. Leaving the door slightly open and praying no one went inside while I was gone, I tiptoed after him. At the corner, I peered round, seeing him disappear up some stairs. I gathered his apartment was on a higher level, maybe only a couple of floors above mine if he wasn't taking the lift.

I kept as far back as I could on the steps so he couldn't see me if he looked down the stairwell. Thankfully, he seemed too pre-occupied to be bothered if anyone was behind him. I glanced up to catch him going through a doorway, so I upped my pace. I waited for a couple of heartbeats before going through the door myself. It brought me out onto a corridor much like the one on my floor except there wasn't a corner, just a wall either end. A longer wall was opposite and in the middle was an elevator.

I walked up to it on shaking legs, immediately spotting that there was only one floor above, going by the lone number that was lit bright green. It made sense that he'd live up there out of the way of other tenants.

I hesitated for a while after the light went out and the lift stopped humming. Then I pressed the button, my stomach rolling over at what I was doing—acting as though I didn't trust him, stalking him into his private space. But I had to know what that phone call had been about and whether I was going to lose the man of my dreams.

The lift hummed again—what if he heard it and knew someone was coming? The doors opened, and regardless of my thought I stepped on board. Prodded the button for the top floor. Closed my eyes and prayed he'd already be inside his apartment and wouldn't be waiting for me as I stepped out of the lift.

The journey was too short. The doors slid wide, and I peered out into another corridor. At the end, a door was ajar so I padded towards it, feeling sick as a pig as my heart hammered. I flattened myself against the wall and looked to the side, into the apartment.

22.

It was more than an apartment.

It seemed to me that it was the penthouse.

What?

The door opened directly onto an enormous living room. Cream carpet lined a sunken square in the middle with wooden flooring on the upper ledges. A black sofa—I'd been right—was fitted against the walls on three sides. Tall windows were to the left and white walls everywhere else. The steps down to the seating area were also carpeted. A fluffy black rug was in the centre, and on that rug stood Blake and Connor.

"The tail wasn't taken off because I didn't trust the promise she'd made," Ginger said. "She's lied before, and I know how much you hate liars and people who break your trust."

Shit. I've done both of those things. Oh, God…

My stomach spasmed.

"And it was good thinking on my part," Connor went on, "because you got yourself a girlfriend and that's dangerous right now—for you and for the new girlfriend."

Dangerous?

He smoothed his orange hair then his bushy eyebrows. "She's obviously been watching you too, otherwise why would someone have been taking pictures? And you really need to let me run a check on this new piece. God knows who *she* is."

"No." Blake stared at him. "I will *not* have her dragged into this."

"She's dragged into it already, just by being with you, brother."

Dragged into what? A daydream scenario popped into my head while Blake and Ginger paced the rug without talking. In my mind, Blake was a drug lord — hence the penthouse — and I could be kidnapped by a rival gang — the woman they were talking about was their leader — which was why this was dangerous. I'd never see Blake, Dad, Jenna or Roo-Roo again, because I'd be hidden in some underground cave — Johnny's basement came to mind — and no one would have a clue where I was.

"Look, pay her off. It's what she's after," Blake said.

"What? She's had enough out of you already. Have you forgotten how she scammed you on that deal? Let me just remind you, shall I?"

"Don't…"

"No, you *need* reminding."

Was Connor about to reveal everything? If that was the case, I'd got lucky by following Blake. I hoped Connor would spill every single bean so I could put my mind at rest — well, a bit more at rest anyway. Not knowing what this was about was doing my head in.

Ginger went on. "I know you were dazzled by who she was. Some famous little slut who offered to be the face of your new venture. And yeah, I can see you wincing, like you want me to shut up, but like I just said, you need reminding. You can't just sweep this under the carpet all the time." He sighed. "You fell for her, didn't you? Or you thought you did. And look where it got you. Two million in the hole because you trusted her when she said it was okay to put her

payment direct from your personal account into hers."
He shook his head. "And I warned you not to do that."
Connor looked smug. "But no, you didn't listen to me."

"Be quiet," Blake said.

"No, I won't, because if you won't look out for
yourself, someone's got to. And that someone's me — as
usual. So, whether you mind or not, I'll carry on. You'll
have to punch me in the mouth like when we were kids
to shut me up, because I'm not going to keep mopping
up after you regarding this *ex* episode."

He sniffed, probably waiting for that punch. Blake
stayed where he was, clearly realising he was better off
just letting his brother rant. And I wanted him to. I
needed the information he was so willing to give.

"Now where was I?" Connor said. "Oh yeah, she
made out that money was a gift and that you still owed
her the original payment." He spat out a laugh. "That's
what company cheques are for. You use them to pay
people and send an invoice along with them. Because
that first payment went through from personal to
personal, it was *seen* as a gift — we couldn't prove a
thing, because she'd persuaded you to your face to give
it to her that way, nothing written down. Your kisses
and your cock clouded your judgement."

So that's why he didn't kiss me for so long.

"Think about what she did — even if it's just to let me
run a check on your new woman." Connor stared at
Blake, obviously waiting for an answer. When he didn't
get one, he carried on. "And there's more. You dragged
your mistake into the courts and for what? To be told
by some judge that the first two mill was accepted as a
gift from boyfriend to girlfriend. You looked a fool and
she came out of it looking innocent. And after that?
She's wanted to hurt you more ever since. So that photo
tonight? Expect repercussions, man."

Oh my God. All this time I thought the photo was about me — Lola mentality right there — yet it's been about him. And four million? What kind of person has four million just floating around like that? Who is he? What does he really do for a living?

The crushing realisation that he'd lied to me too brought a loud sob out of me.

Blake turned to stare at the door.

I whipped myself away from the crack.

"Herman?" he said.

I ran.

And ran until I reached the corner on my floor. I rounded it and…

Blake was already there.

I'd taken the stairs in a mad, crying rush and he must have come down in the lift. I stared at him blocking my doorway. I was trapped with nowhere to go but backwards. Ashamed of my emotions — I couldn't stop thinking of how he'd lied to me, feeling a hypocrite because I'd been just as bad — I swatted the tears off my cheeks and stood there hiccoughing sobs.

"Let me explain," he said, slowly walking towards me.

I backed away. We both had things to explain but I couldn't make myself say that. I held my hands out. "No. You don't need to explain anything. You kept it from me for a reason. I understand."

"No, you don't. How much did you hear?"

"Everything." My bottom lip wobbled.

"But not enough. Please, come inside so I can tell you the whole story."

"This isn't going to work out," I said. "The trust issue…" *Tell him who you are and that by the trust issue you mean him trusting you, not the other way around.* "She was famous and I'm… You don't need famous people in your life. You won't ever trust them again, so us, this, we won't work."

"That doesn't feature for us. You're not famous. I was taken in by her glamour, by who she was. She was supposed to just elevate the business but I thought I fell for her. She seemed to love me. I thought... But since I've been with you, I *know* she didn't love me. Fuck... All this doesn't matter. It doesn't have anything to do with us."

He wouldn't want to know me at all when he found out about Lola. His defences would go up more than ever. Now I knew how he must feel about stars, I couldn't see him ever fully trusting me—and I had to face it that no matter how much he said he loved me, the fact that I'd lied like she had would end us.

I may as well end it now, then, to save him having to do it.

"It'll matter soon," I said. "We should never have got involved. I'll go. You don't need me here. If I'm gone you can deal with this crap without the distraction." *And I can work out how to explain why I lied. I need space to do that.* "I get why you didn't tell me—please believe that. I won't hold it against you. But there are things about me you don't know, and when you find out, you'll think I'm just like her."

"Never." He stepped closer. "Tell me what you mean."

I wanted to, but I really couldn't get the words out. Plus, I was a coward. I didn't want to see his face, to see the hurt there when he found out I was a big fat fibber and he thought I'd been scamming him like she had. Because he'd think that—anyone would.

"No," I said. "You'll find out soon enough." I pushed past him, wishing the contact my hands made with his chest was in different circumstances. I stood in my apartment doorway, one hand on the knob, the other on the jamb, making it clear with my body language that he couldn't come in. "You're going to be hurt—and you'll hate me. But I want you to know that the time I've spent with you has been the best of my life. I need you to believe that. I've kept things back because I wanted you to love *me*. I have no idea what you do for a living but I can guess you earn a lot. I don't know who the hell you are—you must believe that too."

"I love you," he said. "I'll always love you. Please, I don't understand what you're talking about. Tell me, help me make sense of this, because from where I'm standing, you've found out I'm loaded and it's making you run. You've kept things back from me and you think it's going to make a difference to how I feel. What things could possibly do that if you're not famous and not after me for whatever you can get out of me?"

"I'm not here to get anything out of you but…"

"You're going to go back to England early, aren't you?"

I nodded, scrunching my eyes closed.

"Don't do this, Herman."

"I have to. You'll need space. Time…" I opened my eyes. "You'll understand why soon. Maybe in a couple of months." *When my album comes out over here and you see one of the pictures from Austin Powers splashed over CD covers in the shops.*

"This is crazy. I don't know why you can't just tell me now."

"Because I'm a coward. I'm not…who you think I am." That would have to do for now.

"What, you're a prominent photographer, is that it? So what? You think I'm worried you've been sent by her to take pictures of me? Or you're a reporter? Is that what you are? Have you been playing me too? For her?

Getting information she can use to hurt me some more? Fuck!" He slapped one hand against the wall.

"No! Nothing like that. I don't even know who she is. What I told you was true. I came here to find myself. And I found me *and* you. I wanted to be myself with you—my real self—and the longer the relationship went on, the more I wanted to forget...who I am. The more I wanted to be me. And everything back in London—it was like it never happened."

"Dear God, have you been in trouble with the law?"

"No!" *If only it was just that.*

"Because everyone deserves a second chance—so long as you didn't kill anyone or something."

He smiled, to lighten the tension I knew, but I didn't feel like smiling back.

"I didn't kill anyone."

"Stay here. Start a new life. With me."

"I can't. It's not as simple as that. I have commitments, things I can't get out of. Living here isn't possible at the moment. And when you realise who... When you know, you won't want to be with me anyway." *You don't like famous people. Come on, add it up and find the answer so I don't have to say it.* "I have responsibilities."

"Oh...are you married? It doesn't matter. I'll hire lawyers, we'll work it out."

"No, I'm not married. But life isn't as simple as just picking up your life and leading it somewhere else."

"You can make it simple. Only you can put obstacles in your way." He lifted his hands as if to take me in his arms then lowered them down to his sides. "I can see I've lost you already."

"Oh, God, I'm so sorry."

"Does what we have mean nothing to you?"

"It means everything."

"Then stay, for goodness sake! How can it mean everything if you're prepared to walk away?"

"Because— Trust me, you'll know why soon. I'm doing this to save you hurting even more."

I rushed into the apartment and slammed the door. Pressed my back to it and cursed myself for not telling him. I should have just come right out with it so he could be horrified at my fame and know he'd had a close call with me but that we hadn't gone any deeper and he could get over it…us.

It felt ridiculous now, keeping it from him. Stupid that I didn't have the balls to explain. And when he called my name through the door and begged me to let him in, it felt ridiculous again that I didn't open it.

Hi, Blake. You've been duped by another famous person. Well done. Here's a medal.

"I'll always love you," I said. "I never lied about that."

"So let me in." He paused. "What did you lie about?"

"I didn't really lie, I just didn't tell you some things."

"Tell me those things now."

"No. You won't want to know me when you hear them."

"How do you know if you don't give it a try?"

"Because I heard every bit of your conversation with Connor."

"So I don't trust people. I get that you get that. But I trust you. I *know* you love me. You're different to her. The love is different. Your kisses are different."

"Who are you?" I asked, deflecting the focus off me.

"Just some guy in construction."

"Just some guy? What sort of construction?"

"I designed these apartments. And the new football stadium in Texas. Some other places too."

"Blake Hudson... You told me your name but it means nothing to me."

"Blake Hudson—yeah, that's me. The rich guy."

"And you let me think you're just an apartment manager because you thought if I knew you had money I'd want you for that?"

"Yes. I'm sorry."

"Then you should understand my lies," I said. "But I don't want to be here if you don't understand them. I don't want to see the hate on your face."

"I couldn't hate you. Fuck, this is killing me."

I sighed. "I'm already six feet under."

Diary

Dramarama

The thing about being in love is that it makes you do really stupid things. Like flying back to London on the first available flight instead of taking a minute to put your faith in the universe and let fate take care of things.

I'm home. Except I'm not home, because home is where Blake is. Where love and happiness is.

I'm beating myself up for being ridiculous. For running instead of facing the music. I allowed myself to get caught up in my own emotional drama—creating more drama. Unnecessary crap that's proof I'm not ready for a properly serious relationship. I'm too caught up in myself to even admit my lies and try to move on from them. All with the excuse that if he was hurt from what I've done, I'd have seen it on his face.

What a lame excuse!

What about if he wasn't hurt? What if my Lola life didn't bother him because he loves me so much he's prepared to put his past fear of celebs behind him?

What if I've just made the worst mistake of my life?

This Love Thing...

Getting drunk seems the best course of action. Alcohol takes the pain away in situations like this—and when you've broken your own heart. It'll erase the gut-crunching feeling that comes whenever I think of Blake.

I'm a shell. Just skin that's filled with hurt and pain and stupidity and crushed dreams. I'm holed up in my house. No one knows I'm back yet. I can use this time to try to recover—although how can I recover from this? Who can spend their whole adult life wishing for a Mr Perfect, find him, know what it is to truly love and be loved, only to snatch it away from yourself in a moment of foolishness?

And I have been foolish.

So why don't I just find out his email address and rattle out an explanation? Why don't I ring him and babble the words out before he has a chance to stop me?

Pride.

Being ashamed.

Disliking myself for lying in the first place.

Rejection.

The hurt—more hurt than I'm currently feeling.

He hasn't phoned me. And if he loved me, he would.

Doesn't the same go for me? If I loved him, I'd be fighting to keep him.

This love thing... It's harder than I thought. I've made it harder.

Daydreams don't prepare you for twists and turns in the road. They don't explain why you make really divvy decisions, even when you know the answer to it all is just to open your mouth and explain.

That's all I have to do, yet I haven't. I doubt I will.

Why is that?

I don't understand myself.

This.

Anything.

I'm f**ck**

Roo-Roo took my hand and led me onto the dance floor last night. I freaked out to the music as though the song was my favourite and that my bones and muscles had returned and I'm not really filled with all those things I said I was filled with.

I'm Lola. I can't handle this.

I'm Charlotte. I can't handle this.

I'm Herman. I can't handle this.

I'm fucked.

Fate is Cruel

There was an email waiting for me from David. I was

souped up on booze, wrecked by raging emotions, a mess from tears.

The title was: WHAT HAVE YOU BEEN UP TO? NICE MOVE.

I opened it. There were two links inside and a message.

Oh, you're a clever one. He's got a deal to build a music complex in Washington. The last singer he had to be the face of it shafted him—but you knew that, right? What a way to get yourself launched in the US. I could kiss you.

keep seeing him. I'll approach him and set up a deal when you get back.

It seemed as though everyone knew who Blake was except me. I'd been that immersed in my Lola life that I hadn't heard about the music complex or anything Blake has built. Maybe he's famous too but in a different way.

I clicked the first link and realised that Blake is a multi-millionaire. He's built football stadiums, opera houses, homes for the rich and famous.

And I had no idea just how rich or well-known he is.

The second link pulled up *The Huffington Post*. The headline screamed BLAKE HUDSON BAMBOOZLED AGAIN? There's a picture of me and him taken by the snapper. The one where he's kissing me. It hurts to see that.

My fame has been splashed on the virtual page for all to see. For Blake to see. My secret is out, and what makes it worse is David, and now everyone who reads this article, will think I've engineered this. That I've tried to weasel my way into his life by renting one of his apartments. But David rented it.

Oh, God, no. He didn't do that on purpose, did he?

But Blake had come along and asked to help me with my case—I hadn't approached him. Would Blake remember that?

I hope so.

But I imagine all he'll see was what the reporter said. That I was there to get him to use my face so he could launch my US career for me. And I won't blame Blake if he believes that.

The whole episode looks awful. It makes me look awful. A terrible person. And to make it worse, he might think I didn't tell him who I am because I wanted him to fall in love with me before I revealed that I could be the new face to launch the music venue.

Fate is cruel. ☹

Texting Heaven!

I got texts from him today. The first we've shared.

Him: *Why didn't you tell me?*
Me: *Because I want to be loved for me, not who I am.*
Him: *So I'm meant to believe you didn't know who I am?*
Me: *I didn't know.*
Him: *I'm trying to believe that.*
Me: *I'm hoping you can.*
Him: *It's difficult.*
Me: *I'm broken.*
Him: *Me too.*
Me: *What do we do?*
Him: *I don't know.*

Me: *The ball's in your court. But I swear to you, I didn't know. What I told you was true—hard to believe when I lied, I know—and I went to NYC to find myself. My life here... Look up on Google how I became famous. Imagine being shoved into the limelight like that. I was a mess. I still am. But between these messes was a fortnight where I felt more real than ever. We fitted together, didn't we? I miss you.*

Him: *I can't function without you, but this crap... It's in the way. It's stopping me from doing what my heart tells me to.*

Me: *What's that?*

Him: *To trust you. Believe you.*

Me: *I don't blame you if you can't. I wouldn't trust me either.*

Him: *Give me time?*

Me: *To do what?*
Him: *Think.*
Me: *Okay.*
Him: *I still think you're nice.* ☺
Me: *I still think you're awesome.* ☺
Him: *I love you, Herman.*
Me: *I love you, Blake.*

Papering Over the Cracks

A month without contact.

I'm verging on being the Lola the public wants.

Parties. Outrageousness. More parties. Even more outrageousness.

Shipwrecked. My soul is ripped. Got a great big tear in it.

Daydreams bring Mr Law lookalikes.

Taunting me. Showing me what I've let go.

Stupid cow. Stupid, stupid cow.

Time heals all wounds.

Eau de Bullshit. It just papers over the huge cracks. If I walk on them, my heel rips a hole. Wherever I go, the holes will follow, because I carry Blake around with me every step of the way. He's a part of me now. Inside me.

And that's okay. At least that way I'll never be without him.

23

"Tell Roo-Roo all about it," he said, flopping onto my sofa.

I'd avoided Dad and Jenna by texting a note to them that my trip away meant I had to catch up on a lot of things now I was back. If I spoke to them at the moment, they'd hear the distress in my voice and ask what was wrong. I didn't feel up to explaining it to them. They weren't like Roo-Roo, who believed in soul mates and all that sort of thing. And besides, they didn't really understand my Lola Life no matter how hard I tried to explain it to them.

I was just Charlotte in their eyes, the girl they'd always known.

Well, now I had a new name to add to my growing list. Not only was I Charlotte, Lola and Herman but I was Weeping Wilma too.

I curled myself up on the other sofa, wanting to keep my distance so I'd see Roo-Roo coming towards me in plenty of time if he took it upon himself to sidle over and give me a hug. Sympathy would be my undoing, and if I was to get this tale out and off my chest, he needed to steer clear.

I told him what had happened.

"So you just *left* him there with no *explanation*, darling?" His eyes went their usual mega-wideness. "I can't believe you *did* that! What were you *thinking*?"

"I wasn't thinking. Well, I was, but not logically." I twisted my wine glass around. The squeak of it got on my nerves so I stopped.

"Clearly not, petal. So are you going to leave it at the text conversation?" He drained his glass then leaned across to the coffee table so he could get a refill. "You know fate won't have any of that, don't you?" He settled back on the sofa, bringing his legs up so he cuddled his knees with one arm. "If he's your soul mate — and I really believe he is because how can you *love* someone so quickly like you both did? — then he won't be able to stay away from you."

"But can't you see why he'd stay away? That woman really hurt him. I looked it up, read about the case. She really did try to take him to the cleaners." I sipped some wine. Just thinking about the pain she'd caused him made me hurt inside — and the pain I'd caused him.

I'm a bitch and don't deserve him anyway.

"Yes, I can see." Roo-Roo nodded, staring into thin air. "And I see how unfortunate it was that you fell for someone who'd been hurt by another celeb but..." He sighed. "This is a bit of a pickle. A great big gherkin."

I smiled. Trust him to be able to make me do that.

"Life is like a box of chocolates," he quoted. "You just never know what you're gonna get. Or whatever." He waved his hand about. "You know, there is a solution."

I sat up a bit straighter, eager to hear it. "What's that?"

"Why, I could email him, of course. I could tell him how wonderful you are and that you're not a using, conniving little trollop who would want to hurt him."

"No," I said quickly. "That wouldn't work."

"Why not?"

"Because I want him to contact me when he wants to. No forcing it." I shrugged. "By now, he might not even *want* to contact me. He might think I'm too busy and that I don't have the time for him. He might have realised he didn't love me after all. Someone else—"

"No, don't even go there, girlfriend. He has *not* found someone else."

"How the hell would you know?" I stared at him with my mouth open, hoping he hadn't already made contact with Blake without telling me.

"Because I'm sure news of that would have been sent to *The Huff* again. If that woman—that famous strumpet—was prepared to send someone to follow him and snap you two together, she'd do the same again with another woman, wouldn't she?"

"I suppose."

"I do find it odd that he'd be out with another woman in public when she was still sniffing around, though. Don't you?"

I rather hoped he was so happy to be with me he'd wanted to show me off, regardless of the consequences.

Roo-Roo blundered on. "What I think is that he's immersed himself in work to see if he can forget you."

"Is that what you'd do?"

"Isn't that what you've been doing?" He eyed me over the rim of his glass.

"Maybe."

"No maybe about it, you *have* been doing that. And look at you. All tired and raggedy. My word, if he saw you now he'd—"

"He's already seen me at my worst. The bush I told you about, remember?"

"Ah, yes, The Bush Incident. I remember it well. And I must say, darling, it is rather funny when you think about it. Like something out of a comedy movie."

"My whole life is like a bloody comedy movie. I can't seem to get anything right."

"Oh, here we go. Are you going to go down Crying Crescent, take a left down Am-a-Failure Avenue then end up at the Heartbreak Hotel? Please. You're stronger than that. Get those big girl panties on and fight for what you want. Enough's enough, young lady. You've been wallowing for far too long. Bounce-Back Boulevard is waiting for you – if only you'd grow a pair and run down it."

I smiled again – God, he had a knack of making me feel better.

"Take the initiative," Roo-Roo said. "Email him. Even better, give him a ring. He can either ignore the message or decline the call. At least then you'll know he isn't interested. He asked you to give him time. Well, a month is enough in my book."

"But I—"

"No buts." He got up, grabbed my laptop off the coffee table then plonked it on my lap. "Write to him. Ask how he's doing. Nothing heavy. None of that 'Please write back I'm missing you so badly, I need you, I want you, my wotsit has closed up on me' business. Just a straightforward 'How are you?'"

"Roo-Roo! Don't be so gross."

"Well! It *will* close up on you if you're not careful. Or if he's not careful, it'll be open to someone else. Silly man's going to miss the boat if he doesn't hurry up. You can have more than one soul mate in a lifetime, you know."

I couldn't imagine loving anyone the way I loved Blake.

"Go on," he said. "I'll go in the kitchen to give you a bit of privacy."

I opened my email account.

*How much more time do you need? I kind of need to know
your answer before I go mad. Sorry to pressure you.*

I held my breath until my lungs felt like they'd burst.
I looked away from the screen as I let the air out. Stared
at the wall and imagined him reading my email and not
knowing how to let me down gently. Saw him running
a hand through his hair while he worked out what to
say to me in return. How to explain that 'Hey, I'm sorry,
Herman, but I don't love you much after all'.

My text alert pinged.

"Is that him?" Roo-Roo called.

"I wouldn't think so. I emailed him. And I haven't
looked at the text yet," I said.

"Well bloody look then, woman! Good *Lord*!"

I started shaking. Saw his name on my phone screen.
Didn't want to open his message yet I wanted to see it
right now, this second. Why had he texted back instead
of using his email?

Him: *Didn't Connor get hold of you?*

Me: *Connor?*

Him: *I asked him to let you know I'd had an accident at
one of the construction sites. Ended up in traction for three
weeks while they worked out whether I'd done irreparable
damage to my spine.*

Me: *OMG. Are you okay?*

Him: *I am now.*

Me: *I had no idea.*

Him: *Connor has a habit of forgetting to follow my orders.
So, in answer to your question asking how much more time I
need, I'm almost there, Herman. Listen, I have to go. I'll let
you know my answer soon.*

I squealed. Loudly. Roo-Roo came rushing in, his face a big cloud of worry.

"What? Has he told you to go to hell, darling? Oh, he had better not, because let me tell you, I'll be having strong words to say to him if he has. He's got no right to upset my little petal. Tell me his bloody phone number so I can give him a piece of my mind."

He came at me, hands outstretched, fingers like claws.

I gripped my phone so he couldn't take it away from me. "No, you're not having it. He didn't say one way or the other how he felt, but he answered me, and I'm not going to complain about that."

I was giddy with happiness that he'd responded — and so quickly too — but then reality kicked in. What if he *was* going to tell me to go to hell? What if he didn't want anything to do with me — or worse, only wanted to be friends?

"He's been in hospital," I said. "He's been hurt."

"Oh, wow." Roo-Roo thumped down onto the sofa. "Don't I feel hateful now for thinking he'd been ignoring you all this time, leaving you hanging?"

"We both thought that. Connor was supposed to let me know."

"That's the brother, isn't it? The brother who likes all of Blake's girlfriends. Hmm." He pressed a finger to the side of his mouth. "I'm going to take a stab in the dark — and you know how much I like stabbing dark places, darling — and say Connor did that on purpose."

I shook my head. "No, he seems the type who cares for Blake. At least he did when I last saw him."

"Whatever." Roo-Roo did his usual air wave to swat away my suggestion. "So what did Mr Soul Mate have to say? Sharing is caring, dear."

"That he'll let me know his answer soon."

"Ooh, I swear, if he keeps you dangling for much longer I shall have to go over there and bitch slap his face. Really! This is becoming farcical."

"He's been in hospital — didn't you hear me say that?"

"What, and he couldn't drop you a little line? Unless I was in a coma, there is no *way* I would keep the love of my life waiting."

"No one's perfect," I said, knowing I sounded like a typical woman sticking up for her man when her best friend put him down.

"No, they're not, but if he tells you he forgives you, he'd better turn out to be perfect for you. You deserve only the best."

"He is perfect for me." I closed my text messages down, planning to read our conversation again when I was alone.

He called me Herman. That's something, isn't it?

"Right, well…" Roo-Roo bounced off the sofa. "I'm going out to celebrate. Are you coming with me?"

"No. He might contact me again."

"He might. Then again he might not and you'd have wasted valuable Lola in the limelight time. Don't forget you're supposed to be throwing yourself about a bit on the party scene. You have the US to conquer very soon, and I for one want you to succeed there. Delores is in town. *The* Delores? You know, the US sensation? You're meant to be making friends with her, not moping around at home."

"I don't like the idea of making friends with her for my own ends. It isn't right."

"I know it isn't, but it isn't what you know but who you know in this business, and if you want any chance of cracking the US market and to be able to *live* there most of the time, near Blake, then isn't it worth the using?"

Sometimes life decisions were so hard.

"Not tonight," I said. "I will go and meet her, but not tonight."

"Suit yourself, petal. Well, I'm off." He breezed over and kissed my cheek. "Everything will come out in the wash, you'll see. It always does."

The front door slammed as he left. I got up to slip the chain across then went and had a shower. I thought about Blake in there and how awful it must have been to have an accident. What kind of accident had it been? Had he fallen off scaffolding or something? The possibilities were endless, and by the time I got out of the shower I had him mangled, disfigured and walking with two canes.

I dressed in my comfy pyjamas, the ones that were soft like velvet. I bundled myself up in my terry towelling dressing gown then wandered into the living room. I moved to the window to pull the curtains across, noticing a set of headlights, their beams cutting two slices out of the darkness. Roo-Roo must have called a taxi while he'd been in the kitchen.

So was Blake out of hospital or still there? I was dying to ask, and as I sat on the sofa, my laptop on my thighs and my phone in my hand, I resisted messaging him to find out. I put my phone on the coffee table out of my reach. I didn't want to come across as a pesky irritation. I'd said I'd give him time and already I'd broken my promise to myself to leave him alone until he contacted me. If it wasn't for Roo-Roo, I wouldn't have got hold of Blake tonight and known he'd be giving me his answer soon anyway.

I wasn't going to be able to sleep tonight.

One way or another, maybe even by tomorrow, I'd be even more broken-hearted or elated to the point I wanted to burst with happiness.

Time would tell.

And time could be a slow bugger when it wanted to be.

Something tapped, like a branch lightly smacking into a window during a storm. I put the laptop on the sofa and reached for my phone off the coffee table. This wasn't the first time the paparazzi had tricked me into thinking I had an intruder, making me go to the window so they could take pictures.

I walked towards the window—on tiptoe, like someone could hear me coming, for goodness sake—and eased the curtain back a tiny bit. The headlights were gone, but the security light was blazing, which meant someone or something had come close enough to the house to set it off. I frowned, my stomach muscles clenching because hell, I didn't want to have to call the police to deal with another crazy photographer.

The tap came again, and this time I realised it was coming from the front door. I sagged in relief and went out into the hallway.

"Roo-Roo," I called out, "if you've forgotten your bloody jacket again I'm going to brain you!"

I snapped the chain across then flung the door wide open.

"Hello, Herman."

And there he stood.

I stared, unable to believe Blake was there. I had to be imagining it. There was no way he could really be standing in front of me like that. I wanted to cry, to laugh, to scream, to dance.

"What...?" I couldn't finish my sentence.

Blake stared at me, and I wasn't sure how to take the look on his face. It seemed like he was in pain. I clenched my hands into fists to stop myself from reaching out to grab him, to haul him inside. He might not want me touching him. I might repulse him now.

"Are you just going to let me stand here?" he asked.

"Oh, God. Oh, bloody hell. Oh, I…" I couldn't get my mind or body to work properly.

"Well?" He cocked his head. "Will you invite me in so I can give you my answer or not?"

More books from Totally Bound

TOTALLY BOUND — *What's her Secret?*

Sylvie has become part of his soul...

A Girl by Any Other Name

MK SCHILLER

The first in the best-selling
What's Her Secret? Imprint

Everyone tells him he needs to move on, but how
can a man function without his heart?